# Escaping the Blitz

## Jamies Victories

## BOOK TWO

Michael Stevens

A catalogue record for this book is available from the National Library of Australia



**Publisher:**
ASPG (Australian Self Publishing Group)
P.O. Box 159, Calwell, ACT Australia 2905
Email: publishaspg@gmail.com
http://www.inspiringpublishers.com

National Library of Australia Cataloguing-in-Publication entry

Author: Michael Stevens

Title: **ESCAPING THE BLITZ:** JAMIES VICTORIES

**BOOK TWO**

ISBN: 978-1-922792-93-8 (Print)

✧ ✧ ✧

# CHAPTER 1

Jamie was happy to be home again, both he and his brother Al had discovered that some of their old friends were also back after being evacuated, and they had all found plenty to do together during the School holidays.

The boys Father, Captain Ted Dexter had just been posted to Aldershot, so he was now living away from home, which left Di Dexter to manage the family by herself.

Al was a help, but he was only just fourteen and both he and Jamie were always out and about with their friends.

Jerry continued to send his V1 rockets across the Channel, they were not only destructive, but terrifying as well. Di was already regretting bringing the boys home from Dorset, they had been quite happy in the Rectory and much safer than in London. She had been thinking about sending their young Daughter, Beth up to Scotland to stay with her sister Auntie Jean.

All of these thoughts were running through her mind as she lay in bed, tossing and turning, she was worried for her young brood, eventually, she slowly drifted in and out of sleep.

A massive explosion woke her, she sat bolt upright and called out to Al and Jamie.

Both boys ran to their Mum's room and Jamie asked. "Where's Beth Mum?'

Di told him. "She's at a sleepover at Katie's house."

Jamie shouted back at her "Mum, the explosion came from that direction, and I could see flames, I'm going to look for her." he ran out of the room and down the stairs, then into the street, barefoot and still in pyjamas.

Al waited for his Mum to slip into a dress and they followed him.

Jamie arrived, breathless in a street near Katie's house, but he couldn't see what was happening, there were Fire engines, police cars, and dozens of people blocking his view. He was determined to see, so he went down on hands and knees and wormed his way to the front, where he could see that Katie's house and the ones each side had been demolished by the Rocket.

He started to cry, then he forced back the tears and wormed his way back through the crowd, emerging next to a police car, he looked up and saw his Mum talking to an officer. "Mum." he screamed. "The whole house is gone."

Di collapsed into the arms of the policeman, who gently lowered her onto the ground, then the St Johns Ambulance men took over, resuscitating her, and allowing Al and Jamie to comfort her.

More friends and relatives were arriving from nearby to look for their loved ones.

Amongst the chatter, Jamie suddenly recognised a familiar voice, he turned his head and was looking straight at Katie.

"Katie, we thought you were in your house, where's Beth?"

"Right here, behind me, no she's not, she's cuddling her Mum, next to the Ambulance."

Mrs Dexter was holding her daughter so tightly that Beth whispered to her. "Mum, your squeezing the air out of my lungs."

Meanwhile, Katie had explained that earlier that night, their oven wouldn't light because the fuse box had blown, so they all went down to her Aunt Brenda's for Dinner and stayed the night.

After the Dexter's had visited Katie's family at Brenda's house, they trudged home, depressed and sad, as the two families each side had been home when the V1 hit.

Mrs Dexter was now very determined to send all of her three children away from London, until the end of the war.

✧ ✧ ✧

# CHAPTER 2

Jamie and Al were standing on number one platform at Paddington Station, waiting for the Evacuee's Supervisor to tell them to board the train. They had just seen Beth and their Mum off on the train to Scotland, which left from King's Cross Station, now they were going to a country where people spoke a different language, although Wales was really, still part of Great Britain.

Two hours later, Jamie was busy trying to pronounce the names of every station that they had passed. Al cracked up laughing at each attempt, which was annoying the elderly lady sitting in the corner of the carriage. She asked Jamie "Where do you come from with that silly accent Boyo?"

He smiled at her and replied. "London misses."

She shook her head, then turned to look out of the window.

Al laughed and whispered. "You've made a Welsh friend already little brother." Then, the carriage door slid open and the Supervisor entered and told the boys.

"Ours is the next station lads, come into the corridor with your luggage, we will get off here."

The platform was a hive of industry, as children, baggage, and adult carers were busy organising themselves into a column to walk up to the Village Hall.

A group of local lads had gathered at the station, and were escorting the evacuees to the hall, calling out in Welsh, but no one had a clue what they were saying.

Arriving at the Hall, they were given hot drinks and sandwiches, while they waited for their Billets to arrive.

After some time, Jamie and Al were the only ones left. Al murmured to Jamie. "Looks like we might have to catch the next train back home."

As he turned to look for the Supervisor, a large hand fell on his shoulder and Mr Bryn Jones said."You must be the Dexter boys?"

Al quickly replied. "Yes sir, I'm Al, and this is my brother Jamie."

"Pleased to meet you both, sorry we are late but I had to leave work to come here, I'm Bryn Jones and this is my Wife Olwin, we're your Billets."

Olwin Jones told them to "Pick up your bags boys and we'll walk down to our house."

The Jones's lived in a two bedroom cottage on the main street of the village, the boys were shown to their bedroom, which was upstairs, the room was small, and it had a low ceiling which Al found to be a little daunting, as he was quite tall for a fourteen year old, Jamie told him that the cottage was very old and that Welsh people were very small years ago.

"Everyone was short years ago." Retorted Al.

They unpacked their bags and went down to the living room, where Olwin was preparing Tea.

The boys settled in to their new billet quickly, as they were now used to living away from home.

Bryn Jones was a Coal miner, he would get up at five in the morning and be gone all day, when he came home, after Five pm. he was covered in coal dust, as black as the ace of spades. Olwin would prepare a hot bath for him, in a large zinc bath which she would place in front of the fire in the living room, when he was finished they would have dinner, then all went to bed.

Both boys attended the local school, meeting up with some of the children who had been on the train with them. Al, had made friends with a local lass named Wendy, who was the daughter of the village Baptist Minister, he had even managed to sit next to her in class.

Jamie of course, teased him, and told Wendy that Al had girl friends all over England.

The Jones were very strict Baptist's, and the boys had to go to Chapel with them every Sunday, Jamie hated it, but Al got to sit with Wendy, so he was happy.

Being a Coal mining village, there was a huge slag pile adjacent to the railway line, and the local children would climb up it and then slide all the way down, this was one of the only recreations in the Village, as there was a limit of things to do after school.

Al was trying to talk Wendy into joining him and Jamie on the Slag pile slide. She told him. "I used to do that when I was younger, but now, since I've climbed some of the peaks, moun-taineering is much more fun."

"Well, what if we go with you next time you climb?"

"I don't think that Jamie is old enough to climb the local peak, but you and I can go."

Al answered. "On second thoughts, I've just remembered that he doesn't like heights, he'd probably freak out halfway up, or something."

Wendy added. "I'm supposed to help dad on the fundraising stall on Saturday, but we could get up extra early and be gone before anyone knows."

She gave him a list of things that he would need. "Don't say a word to anyone Al, I don't want my Dad to know, OK?"

"Of course Wendy, it's going to be so much fun, just the two of us, up on a mountain."

Jamie, had been sitting watching his big brother talking to Wendy, and he was wondering what they were cooking up, he knew that his brother would be in almost anything for fun, but he was generally too smart to get into trouble, he hoped that this would be the case now.

He strolled over to them, and said. "Let's go for a slide on the Slag heap guys."

Al replied. "That's not much fun anymore Jamie."

"So Al, what are you going to do that is more fun."

Al looked up at the peak which was covered in cloud. And replied "Wendy and I might go to the library."

"Wow Al, that's really exciting, you gunna read horror books together?" Wendy gave him a withering look, then told Al that she had to go home and prepare stuff for the parish fund raiser, with that she quickly ran of towards the Manse.

"What's wrong with Wendy Al?"

"Nothing nosey, why?"

"What were you two talking about for so long, you going to elope with her?"

"Stop asking silly questions Jamie, I'm going back to the billet, it's tea time, coming?"

Jamie followed his big brother home, all the time wondering what those two were up to.

There was an amateur climbing club in the village, as it was surrounded by tall mountains, and they were rugged up near the peaks, covered with large rocks, and climbing them required skill and a lot of local knowledge.

The clubhouse was situated a few hundred yards from the village, and the members all kept their equipment there, which some of them shared when they were climbing.

Wendy was a member of the club and she had become a strong climber, but she was always accompanied by a more experienced member, usually her big Brother, Stewart.

Saturday morning, which was usually the time for the villagers to sleep in or just have a lay in, but not this Saturday,

Olwin Jones was rudely awakened by a loud banging on the front door, she hurried down to see who was responsible for the noise.

"For goodness sake Pastor, what is so urgent? Bryn is resting from a hard weeks work."

"Have you seen my daughter Wendy, Mrs Jones?"

"No, not this morning Pastor."

"She's supposed to be helping me on the stall today, but she's nowhere to be seen."

"Young lasses do as they please nowadays, Pastor, but she was here late last night, talking to Al."

"I need to see Al, now."

Olwin called out. "Al, come down and talk to the Pastor, please."

Jamie shouted back to her. "He's not here Mrs Jones, he must have gone out very early."

"You see, Olwin, these London boys are trouble, he's abducted my daughter, I'm going to the Police station now."

Jamie, quickly dressed and started to search for Al and Wendy, he was sure that they were up to something, but he knew that Al would never do anything illegal.

He searched the bedroom and noticed that Al had taken his torch and his Anorak, as well as gloves and a water bottle, he decided that they must be going on a hike, but why the secrecy? He knew that Al wanted to climb a peak in the district, but he had no idea how to do it, he could ask Wendy, as she was a climber, surely they wouldn't climb alone, he thought.

He went looking for Stewart, hoping that he would be at the Manse, he saw him setting up a stall, he asked him. "Stewie, which way would you climb the Tor on a day like this?"

"Jamie, you are not going up there today, or any other day."

"No Stewie its not for me, its about an English paper at School, I have to describe a way up the mountain."

"OK, well It looks like there's a storm coming in, so I'd take the left side, you get cover from the wind over there and you can hide in those caves in bad weather, but don't you even think about going up there."

Jamie thanked Stewart and went home to get his parka and water bottle, put on his boots, then set off up the Tor.

Pastor Williams was pacing up and down in the Police station, a road accident in the main road had both officers occupied with the injured parties and the police reports.

"I'll go and look myself, constable, no thanks for your help." and with that he stormed out of the station, while continuing to rant about the lack of help.

He finally gave up looking, and decided that he had to go and organise the fund raiser, being the leader of the church, so he went home to the Manse and told his wife Ann that he would continue to look for Wendy and Al after the Market.

Al, and Wendy were approaching the point in the pathway, where climbers had to choose which way to proceed. "Al, I think we should go left, as I can see clouds building up, and the wind has changed."

"We can always go back Wendy, we can try again tomorrow."

"My dad won't let me out of the house for a month after this, so we go up now."

They continued to climb, and with the weather changing rapidly, as it does on most mountains, Al started to get a bit worried, but he just pushed on, hoping that his trust in Wendy's ability was not going to get them into trouble, also he didn't want her to see that he was concerned.

They passed a huge cornice and turned South, the wind from that side virtually blew them over, it was also freezing cold, it was straight off the Irish Sea.

It had started to rain heavily and they were both wet and cold, Wendy pulled Al into a crevice between two large rocks, and they sat together and tried to keep warm, by holding each other.

Meanwhile, Jamie was struggling up the mountain, against the wind and rain, he was also saturated, but he was determined to get his brother to return home.

After some time while struggling up towards the craggy rocks, he could hear a voice calling out, he looked back and saw who he thought might be Stewart, climbing up behind him, and waving, he stopped and waited for Stewie, who soon caught up with him.

"Jamie are you mad? I could see you with my binoculars back at the clubhouse, what are you trying to do? Whatever it is, you're not doing it on my watch today, so let's go back down and get warm at the Club."

"Stewie, Wendy and Al are up there and they must be in trouble."

Stewart looked at the boy and said. "What? They are crazy, you're right, we will need more help, we can't do this on our own, I'll go down and get my mates at the Club to join us, but you must stay right here, and don't move till I get back with the boys."

Jamie nodded.

Stewart then descended as fast as he could down towards the Club house. Jamie watched Stewart disappear into the driving rain, then he continued to climb towards the Rock face up ahead, where he might find somewhere to shelter from the rain and wind.

Wendy and Al were huddled together in the crevice, he asked Wendy. "What's that flapping noise, it's coming from the windward side."

"It sounds like a sheet flapping on the line."

"Who dries their washing on a mountain in a rainstorm Wendy?"

"If your worried smarty, go and look for yourself."

"I can't stand it, I'm going to have a peek."

Al, climbed around the large rock that was protecting them from the wind and rain. He cried out to Wendy. "There's a body here Wendy, come and see, it's wrapped in some sort of material."

Wendy scrambled around to him, and saw the figure laying face down. "That's a parachute he's covered in Al, turn him over."

"It's a Jerry uniform Wendy, I'll check to see if he's breathing."

Al pulled the parachute away from the body and checked his pulse. "He's alive alright, he's coming round, Wendy get on the other side of the rock, he may have a gun."

The injured parachutist groaned, then turned to look at Al. "Vere is this?"

Al replied. "You are on a mountain in Wales. We want to help you, please don't shoot us."

The injured man nodded and pointed to his right leg. "Broken I think."

"Is it painful." Al inquired.

"Very" he replied, then grimaced in pain.

Wendy said. "Al, you have to take his weapons, he might do something crazy, if he becomes delirious."

Al then searched the airman, who did not resist, but was looking at a pouch in his uniform. "Drugs." He said, and then pointed to his apparently broken leg.

Wendy realised that it was Morphine, found the needle, and smartly injected him in the leg.

He thanked her profusely, in his native tongue, she smiled back at him, and watched his eyes slowly close.

Jamie had reached the Crevice in the rocks and had seen the two backpacks unattended, he thought the worst, surely they hadn't gone up without their gear.

Then he heard Wendy's voice, he climbed round to the other side, and saw Al holding a gun.

"Al, put it down." he shouted.

Al turned to see his little bother, saturated and obviously frozen, giving him orders. but he did put the gun down, then embraced Jamie. "How did you know where we were?"

"I put two and two together, and guessed that you would be climbing today." then he indicated the injured airman, "It was on the news, the German plane crashed into the sea early this morning, he must have been here all night poor devil."

Wendy told him. "He's got a broken leg, we have to get him down the mountain, somehow and quickly."

Jamie chirped. "Help is on the way, Stewart went down to get his mates to come up and get you two."

"You told my brother where I was, how could you Jamie."

"You should thank me Wendy, Stewart told me how to find you."

They continued to argue, Al shouted. "Quiet, I can hear someone calling, it must be the searchers."

He and Jamie stood away from the rocks waving and shouting.

Within minutes, Stewart and five of his burly mates rounded the corner, complete with ropes and a sled.

Stewart took possession of the gun, and scolded both Wendy and Al, for being so stupid, he then had his mates load the injured airman onto the sled, then the party slowly descended towards the clubhouse.

The Police Sergeant and Pastor Williams were waiting in the clubhouse, both extremely angry about the fiasco.

Club members helped the weary party into the rooms, helping them to take off their saturated clothing and taking them to a huge fire to warm up and dry their clothes.

The Sergeant told both Wendy and Al. "What you did was totally irresponsible, what went on in your head young Wendy Williams?"

Her Father then tore into Al, screaming at him. "You abducted my daughter and you will go to jail." Stewart intervened between his Dad and Al. "It wasn't his Idea father, don't blame him, he wasn't abducting Wendy at all, he's a schoolboy, go home and leave everything to the Policeman."

This made Williams even worse, he continued to rant at the boys until the Sergeant told him to go home.

He walked away mumbling and cursing.

An ambulance had arrived to take the German Pilot to hospital, the Sergeant accompanied him until the Military Police arrived.

The man from the local paper was busy taking photographs and asking all sorts of question.

After warming up and having hot drinks and snacks, Al and Jamie, walked home to their Billet.

Wendy was angry at her father and told Stewart that she didn't want to go home.

He told her that he would go with her and if their Dad started in on her he would not let him harm her, but she must take some blame for what they did.

Al and Jamie arrived back at their Billet, much the worse for wear, cold, wet and unhappy about the attitude of the Pastor, who vowed, never to allow his child near another Londoner.

Bryn and Olwin Jones, were most unhappy with the boys, Williams had gone straight there from the clubhouse, and embellished the tale with a whole pack of lies, he had recommended that the boys be returned to London as soon as possible, labelling them a danger to local children.

The following day, Stewart called in to say goodbye to them, and he told Al, that Wendy had said that she was going to write to him, then asked them to please forgive his Father for his nasty attitude, he also thanked Jamie for being smart enough to seek them out, and organise help.

Once more, the boys were standing on a platform, waiting for a train, Olwin and Stewart waved them off, and they prepared themselves for the reception that awaited them in London.

✧ ✧ ✧

# CHAPTER 3

On their return Home to Greenwich, both boys were busy competing with each other in trying to explain to their Mother about the incident in Wales.

Di Dexter was not amused by the mountain climbing effort, and very upset by the letter that Pastor Williams had sent her, with Al, a copy of which he had forwarded to the person responsible for billeting children. Apparently Al was no longer permitted to go anywhere as an evacuee.

This was extremely upsetting for Di as she wanted the boys out of London again because the V1 bombs were still arriving, often enough to terrify everyone.

Nevertheless, life slowly returned to normal, that is 'War normal'.

Al had been accepted into Colf's Grammar school on a sports scholarship. Jamie being less of an athlete, attended Greenwich Secondary Central School, which was just two blocks along the main road, his Dad had also gone there.

He could walk to school each day, and sometimes he would come home for lunch.

On one sunny January day, he had taken advantage of having a home lunch and was on his way back to school, he walked towards the bridge that crossed the railway line, he heard a strange squealing noise, it sounded like a flock of birds, but it wasn't, it was an aeroplane.

Jamie saw it appear to his right, flying low over the railway line, he thought at first that it was a Spitfire, and started to wave at the pilot, who he could clearly see in the cockpit.

Then he saw the Black cross on the side of the fuselage, it was a German Fighter-bomber, and it was spurting orange flames out of its cannons.

He turned and ran as fast as he could back home.

Bursting into his front door he shouted. "Mum, there's a Jerry plane firing its cannons."

Di Dexter ran from the kitchen and hugged her son, saying. "I saw it, and it's dropped a bomb near the school."

She led him towards the door and said. "We have to go and see the damage, it might have hit the school."

They hurried on foot towards the school, following others who had seen and heard the Plane.

Jamie left his mother to talk to the other parents who had children in the school, he slipped past the Warden and went in a side door, running straight into Mr Lyle, the English teacher. "What are you up to Jamie?" he asked, then followed up with. "It's OK lad, there are a couple of teachers with a few with cuts and bruises but no one is seriously injured, the bomb landed in the playground at the back, you can go home now and we will see you here tomorrow morning."

The good news quickly spread throughout the crowd, and they dispersed, Jamie and Di walked home in silence, as she was thinking what might have happened.

Two things preyed on her mind, had Jamie left home a few seconds earlier, he would have been on the bridge, directly in line of the gunfire, secondly, the bomb could easily have fallen on the school itself, killing dozens if not hundreds of children.

On the news that night, they heard that a Flight of German Focke Wolf 109 fighter bombers had flown up the railway lines in south London and bombed a number of schools, and the toll was in its hundreds of children and dozens of teachers killed and injured.

Di Dexter was now frightened for her sons safety, she was determined to find them another billet, she spent several hours ringing the authorities, but none would give Al permission to go to an official billet.

Jamie on the other hand had been lucky, he was allocated a billet in Etchingham in Sussex, so he was already packing his bags once again.

$$\diamond \;\; \diamond \;\; \diamond$$

# CHAPTER 4

Jamie had done all of this before, in the past with his brother Al, now he was on his own.

Di Dexter had waived him goodbye at Charing Cross station, an hour later and he was standing outside the Station in Etchingham, he had been told to wait there for his new Billet.

He watched the locals going about their business, each one giving him an enquiring look as they walked past. He imagined that they were saying to themselves, "What is that school boy with a huge suitcase doing here?"

But of course they only saw him as a stranger, as everyone knew everyone else in Etchingham.

He was aroused from his reverie by a huge black car stopping next to him, he looked at it, it was shiny and very posh, it was a Bentley.

A mans voice assaulted his ears. "Young Man, are you master James Dexter by any chance?"

Jamie squeaked. "Yes sir, yes sir."

"Then place your suitcase in the back seat of my car and climb in next to me."

"Yes sir"

Jamie sank into the passenger seat of the Bentley, he looked up at the driver, and said "I'm Jamie Dexter and I'm from Greenwich Sir."

"Love Greenwich, you are lucky to live there my boy, but back to business, So its Jamie not James, is that correct?"

"Yes sir."

"Jamie, I am Colonel Robertson M.C. Retired, you will be living in my house as a guest, my housekeeper Mrs Lawton will take care of you and all of your needs, I am a busy man most of the time, but I will give you my attention in the evenings, should you need it, you know, schoolwork and that stuff. Now I have to get back to feed my pets, so hold on to your seat, I can be a demon on the road".

They arrived at the Mansion in just a few minutes, and Jamie was convinced that the Colonel could be a demon alright. They both alighted and Jamie took his large suitcase and gas mask out of the back and followed this huge man inside.

They were greeted by a pleasantly plump Mrs Lawton, who gave Jamie a massive cuddle and squealed. "He's gorgeous Colonel, but he needs fattening up, I'll attend to that, come now dear boy, I'll take you up to your suite."

Jamie was a little alarmed at the reception by both adults, and now he was climbing the huge winding staircase up to the first floor, clinging to the banisters, as the walls were covered with animal pelts, huge animals, firstly a brown bear, then an arctic fox and at the top of the stairs a cheetah, all of them complete with eyes and teeth.

They entered a huge bedroom. "This is yours, Jamie." purred Mrs Lawton. "You can choose your own bed, and wardrobe, that door leads to your bathroom, now drop your bag, you can unpack later, right now we are going to my kitchen, where you will fill your tummy and you will tell me all about yourself."

The happy lady took him by the hand and they walked down the staircase with Jamie on the Bannister side again.

In the kitchen she told him that he was to call her Betty, as they were now buddies.

Jamie was trying his best to absorb everything that had happened since standing outside the Train station, did the Colonel mean the animals on the wall when he said feed my pets? Also he had never been cuddled by anyone the way Betty did.

She produced a plate of cold meat, cheese, lettuce, tomatoes and crusty bread and butter, then told him. "I've made a fresh batch of cakes for you, they are in this jar, you must help yourself whenever you are hungry, you're a little on the slim side dear boy."

She then spent the whole time listening to his life story, as he tucked in to the plate of food.


He was lying in the bed that he had chosen, the one furthest from the door, just in case one of the Colonels pets wandered in, where he could climb out of the window.

The house was the poshest place he had ever seen, everything was immaculate, the towels were pure white and embossed with the Colonels family crest.

He wished that Al was with him, as he was a bit concerned about Betty and her cuddles.

He drifted off to sleep, thinking about the Black Bentley, what a great car, he wondered if he would get more rides in it.

He awoke, startled by a loud voice calling up the staircase. "Rise and shine my boy, we have work to do." Ordered the Colonel. Jamie quickly threw on his clothes and ran down the stairs.

"I didn't mean that quick Jamie, you need a hearty breakfast first boy, then we'll tackle my pets." Barked the Colonel, leading him into the dining room, where Betty had laid out a full cooked breakfast for each of them, with hot slices of toast as well.

Jamie had never eaten a full cooked breakfast before, and he was struggling with one of the two sausages left on his plate.

The Colonel barked. "Leave those Jamie, Betty has over-loaded your plate, she does it all the time. We have to feed the pets now, so come with me, ever seen a Mink before Jamie?"

"A what Sir?"

"Obviously not eh? Just open that sliding door for me please and don't mind the smell."

Jamie did so and the aroma knocked him back a bit but it was not as bad as some animals make, he looked around the massive shed, it was in pristine condition, everything in order and very clean, just like the house.

He was led to the first cage, his Host took the lid off and reaching inside lifted a pure white animal out, holding it's mouth closed with his fist. "Don't try to do this Jamie, until you are competent, Mink have probably the sharpest teeth in the animal world, and they will bite."

"It's beautiful Colonel, I've never seen an animal as white as this."

"I will teach you all about them in good time, but right now we have to clean their cages, put fresh straw in, then feed and water them."

"How many are there Colonel?"

"Probably close to one hundred and thirty, I've just shipped twenty down to London."

"It will take us all day sir."

"No it won't boy, Rogers will be here soon, he does it every day for me, I just wanted you to be aware that they are here, just joking about the work, young fellow."

"I can hardly move after that breakfast Colonel, I'm only used to cornflakes and milk."

"You're a country gentleman now Jamie, need to fatten up. By the way do you play Golf?"

"I've never even seen a golf club before."

"I'll teach you, we'll go on Sunday, OK."

"Yes Colonel, but what about Church?"

"Bugger Church, never had time for it, spent most of my life in India, never had Church there, just fought the locals, fine soldiers, Indians."

"My parents are Atheist Colonel so they wont mind if I miss."

"Good Jamie, we are on the same page lad, now here comes Rogers to do some work, we'll disappear."

Jamie had taken a liking to the Colonel, he had sorted out the breakfast menu with Betty, she was a little reluctant to comply, but a word from her boss convinced her that it would so be.

Jamie attended the local school, and easily made friends, as everyone was aware that he was living with local 'Royalty', that being the Colonel, his family the Robertson's had been the feudal landowners since the seventeen hundreds, and had owned most of the land in and around the Shire.

Because Jamie had been taught to speak English well, by his parents, both Di and Ted Dexter were English teachers by profession, and insisted on their children speaking well. Therefore the local children, assumed that he was a bit posh like the Colonel, perhaps they were probably related or something, so they included him in all of their games.

The Colonel was busy telling Betty to stop mollycoddling Jamie. He told her. "He's a big boy, just short, that's all, he's not a baby and he has family back home."

She retorted. "He hasn't told you about his big brother has he?"

"What, he said he has a sister called Beth."

"They both have a big brother called Al."

This information slightly upset the Colonel, as he had believed everything that the boy had told him, but he obviously had a reason to hide the fact that he had a brother.

He asked Betty. "What do you know about this brother?" "Jamie was going to tell you, but I told him not to."

"Out with it Betty."

"OK sir, he has been banned from the Evacuee list, and Jamie thought that if you knew you might send him home."

Just then, Jamie walked in the front door from school, and said. "I'm home." The Colonel called back. "In my office now young man."

Jamie, shuddered, he had not been spoken to like this before, he quickly obeyed his angry host. "Yes sir what is it?"

"Sit down and start telling me about Al."

Some twenty minutes later Jamie and Betty left the office and went to the kitchen for a cuppa and cake, both were smiling and Jamie was very relieved.

The Colonel was on the telephone to Rector Ellicot. "You old devil Ellicot, still up to charity work, taking in dozens of young evacuees."

"Good to hear from you Sir, been a long time, how did you know about my guests?"

"Aha Rector, please tell me about the Dexter boys."

"Certainly sir, two of the nicest young boys that I have had stay here, I can recommend them to anyone, particularly you Sir.

The Colonel smiled at the phone. "Ellicot, that was what I wanted to hear, thank you old chap, I'll see you at the next Regimental Annual dinner, good bye."

He then put the phone down, and bellowed out. "That Pastor was a Liar, I'll have his hide, come here boy, we are going to ring your Mother."

# CHAPTER 5

Di Dexter was on the telephone, seeking permission to send Al away from the City. She was reminded of the episode in Wales, which she said was misconstrued by Pastor Williams.

One evening, while she and Al were sitting, listening to the radio, there was a knock on the door, she asked who was there?

A girls voice answered politely. "Wendy Williams and my Brother Stewart Mrs Dexter, please can we talk to you?"

Al heard her voice, he quickly ran down to his mother and said. "Mum, they've come all the way from Wales just to talk to you, please let them in."

"Al, for goodness sake, of course they can come in, just open the door son." He let the Williams siblings in and shook hands with Stewart and hugged Wendy, then he introduced them to his mother.

She asked Stewart. "Why did you travel all the way to London, it's no place to be at this time."

Stewart replied. "We wanted you to know the truth about the mountain climbing incident Mrs. Dexter."

After hearing Stewart and Wendy's version of the incident, she said. "Your Father is not a very nice person, Stewart. I don't believe that Al did anything wrong, now he can't be evacuated."

Mrs Dexter none of it was Al's fault, we tried to tell dad but he just wanted Al to be away from Wendy, so he told a pack of lies to the police."

"How come he let you both out of his sight?"

"He has left our home and the village, Bryn and Olwin Jones told the church elders that he lied to the police, so they sacked him."

"So, where is he now Stewart?"

"He took the Parish Van and has disappeared into thin air."

"Your mother must be devastated."

"No she's very happy and so are we."

Di then told them. "You must stay over for a few days while we contact the Billeting office and you can tell them your story."

Then she and Wendy went into the kitchen to prepare a meal for them all. Stewart and Al were chatting about Mountain climbing, when the telephone rang.

Al answered it and heard Jamie's voice saying, "Al, I want you and Mum to talk to The Colonel, it's very important."

Di ran to the phone and answered. "Mrs Dexter here sir, is everything OK?"

He answered. "Don't be alarmed madam, I have your son right next to me and he is beaming, I rang you to let you know that Pastor Williams is a confounded liar, I have spoken to Rector Ellicot, who had nothing but praise for your two boys, so, would you allow me to bring Jamie up on Saturday to pick up Al, there is a billet waiting for him in Etchingham."

Di was overjoyed, she hastily agreed with him and told Al, Wendy and Stewart the good news.

Jamie was shuffling his feet, while waiting for the Colonel, he was keen to get going, as they were on their way to London to pick up Al.

He noticed that the Great room door was slightly ajar, he had been told by Betty not to go in there, which of course he had obeyed, now he was itching to go and just have a peep, he lent sideways and looked in, then recoiled in horror. "Oh! what is that?"

The Colonel, had just walked out of his office and saw Jamie falling backwards onto him. "Whoa, little fellow, what's wrong?"

Jamie looked up at him, thinking that he was in trouble. "Sorry Sir the door was open and I just had to have a look. I know I'm not allowed in there, I won't do it again, ever."

The Colonel smiled, picked him up and gently propelled him into the vast room. "Just a few of my trophies, Jamie, of course you can look at them, they wont bite."

The boy was amazed at the sight before him, covering most of the floor were a variety of Animal furs. Complete with head, eyes and teeth. He took particular notice of the huge Kodiak Bear, which had been staring at him as he had peeped in the door. There was a Polar bear and a Black bear as well, and lying in front of the fire place was a Bengal Tiger, he wandered around looking in wonder at all of the Trophies, including the animal heads complete with antlers adorning the walls.

The Colonel in his usual commanding voice told him. "Jamie, you can continue the inspection when we return from London, come now, the Bentley awaits.

Al and Wendy were waiting in the front garden of the Dexter house, when the Black Bentley pulled up.

Al saw Jamie sitting in the front seat, and asked him. "Do you think that you're Royalty little brother?'

To which Jamie replied. "You will have to get used to it Al, we are royalty in Etchingham."

The Colonel had already introduced himself to Di, Stewart and Wendy. and Al was formally greeted by his new host.

"You're not the little demon that Williams said you were." Barked the Colonel.

Wendy quickly informed him. "Al's one of the nicest young men that I've ever known Colonel."

He smiled at her and said. "Of course he is Wendy, but you might be a little bit biased?"

She laughed and answered him. "I suppose so sir, we were alone in a blizzard on the Mountain for a long time, he is very caring."

Di Dexter interrupted the sweet talk, by saying. "We all need a cup of something warm and some cake, now let's go into the lounge and discuss what's next."

They spent some time bringing Colonel Robertson up to date on Pastor Williams disappearance, then he told Di that he knew her husbands Commanding Officer, and he might be able to get Ted a transfer back to London.

Then he offered Wendy and Stewart a lift to Paddington Station, which they politely declined as Di had asked them to stay for a while, because she wanted to know more about their home town in Wales.

Then it was time for them to leave, and Di said her goodbyes to both her sons and tearily waived them off.


Back in Etchingham, Al was given a guided tour of the Mansion, which left him in awe, after which he was taken to the Mink Farm, where Jamie told him that they were to clean the cages every day.

Al recoiled in horror, saying. "No way, you said it was all fun here." Jamie laughingly told him. "Just joking Al, Mr Rogers does all of the hard work here, but we have to help the Colonel when he sells off some skins."

Betty had met Al and she was overjoyed to have another lovely young man to fuss over, and told him that he too needed fattening up.

Al soon fell into the routine at the manor, and went with Jamie to the local high school, where he soon made friends with the local lads, and one particular girl, Beryl Baker.

It was soon school holidays, and Mr Rogers had asked the Colonel if he could take two weeks off, and take his family to Hastings for a beach side holiday.

While he was away the boys were to take on his duties at the Farm.

They enjoyed working together, and got through each job quickly, leaving them time to go with the Colonel to the Golf Club, where they quickly picked up enough skills to play a round or two.

On the Monday morning of the second week of the holidays, Jamie was sent to buy bread rolls from the Bakery, the Bakers daughter, Beryl, who was serving customers at the time, asked Jamie what he wanted.

He told her, "Six bread rolls please, Beryl and why is your Dads Van parked up near the Manor, no one takes bread up there?"

"My Dad's van is in the garage Jamie and here are your rolls."
"I saw it Beryl, parked on the side of the road just now."

"Jamie, what colour was it?"

"Sort of Creamish."

"Dad's van is White with 'Bakers Bakery' written on the side and it's in the garage."

"Oh, then it's not yours."

Beryl, couldn't help herself from teasing him, she said. "It might be a German spy watching you Jamie. Better keep your room locked at night."

He retorted."I'm not afraid of spies, Beryl, I caught one in Dorset."

"You are a liar, Jamie Dexter, How could you catch a spy? I'll ask Al about it"

"Is my brother your boyfriend Beryl?"

She flicked her apron at him over the counter, saying. "Get out of here you pest."

He quickly left the shop, as he had seen Mrs Baker coming through the back door.

He then ran all the way back to the Manor, to tell Al about Beryl's tantrum. As he walked into the Manor driveway he spotted the van again.

The next morning they were cleaning the Mink cages, as Al walked past the side entrance, he knocked the door with his bucket and it flew open.

He shouted out. "Jamie you left the side door unlocked yesterday morning, I just knocked against it and it flew open."

Jamie replied. "No Al, I worked on the other side yesterday, you did this side."

"So I did." said Al, in alarm. "Then who would have opened the door."

Jamie whispered. "Don't tell anyone Al, but it might have been me on Sunday, remember I spilt a bucket near that door, and had to swab out. But I was sure that I closed and locked it."

Al assured him that it was OK, he locked the door when they had finished and they ran off to meet the Colonel and get a lift to the Golf Club.

Following their round of Golf, on the way home, they passed by the Van, on the side of the road, Jamie quickly memorised the plate number, just to check that it wasn't Beryl's Dad's van.

The next morning, bright and early, the boys went down to the Farm and started work, first taking the Mink out of their cage, cleaning each cage and putting fresh straw down, then putting each animal back. This took some time as Mink have exceptionally sharp teeth, and need to be handled with care.

Jamie was removing the babies, as they had to be cleaned everyday. He asked Al. "How many babies were there yesterday?"

Al replied, "Four in that cage and four in the other, Why?"

Jamie shouted. "Al, there's four little guys here, but the other cage is empty."

Al quickly answered. "Perhaps Mr Rogers came back last night?"

Jamie cried out. "No Al, go and tell the Colonel, someones been here, there are some cages missing altogether."

Betty heard the Colonel bellowing out loudly, giving instructions to Al and Jamie, yelling at her to ring the police immediately, then to ring Rogers at Hastings and get him back here.

Both boys were busy checking which animals were missing, and feeling very guilty about it all.

The police sergeant had arrived accompanied by a policewoman, who was asking everyone questions about the theft. She almost had Jamie in tears as she was virtually accusing the boys of being involved in the theft.

The Colonel told her. "Don't be bloody stupid, girl. These boys are of excellent character, and have helped the authorities in the past themselves."

Rogers arrived later and quickly helped in supplying a list of missing animals to the Sergeant, and likely places, where they could be sold.

Colonel Robertson was besides himself, he had never had anything, let alone an animal stolen from him.

The Police Sergeant was now asking how long had the boys been living there. Robertson exploded once again, saying. "Get the real criminals, what do you think these lads would do with my Mink?"

Thankfully, the police Inspector arrived and sent the uniformed officers back to the station.

"Now Rogers, where are they likely to sell these animals?" asked the Inspector. Rogers answered. "Probably Oxford, there have been some stolen animal pelts sold around that area of late."

"Right Colonel, we'll concentrate our search in Oxford, We'd better head off now while the scents fresh."

Jamie, sang out. "Inspector, perhaps you should take a note of this registration number, its off a Creamy coloured Van, that's been lurking in this road for a few days lately."

Robertson bellowed out. "Why the devil didn't you tell me lad?"

"I thought it was the Bakers van, until Beryl told me that it couldn't be, it's the wrong colour."

The Colonel ruffled Jamie's hair and thanked him for being smart enough to get the number of the vehicle, then both he and Rogers joined the Policeman on the trip to Oxford.

Al and Jamie went back to finishing cleaning up in the Farm, now pleased that they had been exonerated. Al told Jamie. "I'm going straight down to see Beryl, and tell her about that Van being involved in the robbery, she might have to give you an apology Jamie."

"Yes Al, and tell her that I did help catch a spy in Dorset, because she doesn't believe me."Jamie taunted.

Al, jibed. "Are you going to be unbearable again, Detective Dexter."

Then he jumped on his bike and peddled off to the Bakery, using this, as an excuse to see his girl.

Jamie, having finished in the Mink Farm, went to the kitchen to have a chat with Betty, who produced the jar of cakes, and they both sat and tucked in while she told him what a smart lad he was.

Later that afternoon, The Colonel and Mr Rogers, returned triumphantly to the Manor, the police at Oxford had arrested the Driver of the Van, by checking the number plates of all of the similar vehicles in the town, when they caught him, he still had all of the Mink on board, uninjured and all were well.

Jamie asked. "Where are the Mink Sir."

"The police are holding them, they are going to set a trap for the gang who sell the pelts on to other dealers." Rogers told him. "And by the way Jamie, the Superintendent at Oxford wanted your name, so it might appear in the local paper this week."

Al cried out in agony. "Oh no, please, I can't stand this Colonel, I'll go and stay in the Golf Club until he gets over it."

Jamie jumped in with a request. "No Al, please stay and help me and Mr Rogers with the Mink, I promise that I won't brag about it to anyone."

Al responded jokingly, with. "OK. One word about the robbery and I will go back to London."

# CHAPTER 6

Al was glad to be back at school again, where he was the centre of attention, due to his sporting prowess.

Jamie, on the other hand was keeping a low profile, spending his time in the school library, that is were he was going on the second morning back at school.

Beryl saw Jamie heading to the library and followed him inside.

"Jamie Dexter, I owe you an apology, you're not a liar, actually you're a hero, Al told me all about the Rectory and your time in Dorset, you are quite a nice boy, nearly as nice as your big brother Al."

"You're right Beryl, Al is nicer than me, I'm the nosey one, and that gets me into trouble."

"So, are we friends Jamie?"

"Of course Beryl, we always were."

"Good, then will you come down to our holiday house in Hastings next weekend, with Al?"

"Yes, I love the beach, thanks Beryl."

With the school bell ringing in their ears, both of them went to their classrooms. Jamie with a huge smile on his face.

At dinner that night, Al asked Jamie. "Why did Beryl ask you down Shrimp?"

"I'm not a shrimp. I am a human being, just a short one, and Beryl and I are friends again, It's OK Al, I can sit with the her Folks while you and her canoodle."

Betty interjected. "Now boys, don't fight over a girl, there are plenty in the village who would like to meet you two."

"Beryl is Al's girl Betty, I don't need one, they can hold you back." Jamie quipped, then he approached The Colonel. "Sir, do you have any binoculars that I could borrow on the weekend."

"I'm sure that I have several pairs, and a spyglass Jamie, take your pick, you might even spot a smuggler or a pirate or two."

Al chipped in."Just don't spy on me and whoever I'm with."

The Colonel told them that he would drive them down to Hastings on Friday after a nine holes of golf.

The boys then prepared for their weekend at Hastings, Jamie gathering his espionage equipment, together with two pair of binoculars. Al was carefully packing his poshest casual clothes, deodorant, etc. and new bathers.

At Golf on Friday, Al soundly beat Jamie and continued to give him tips on how to improve his game on the way down to Hastings in the car. Robertson dropped them off at the Baker's holiday home, then hurried back to Etchingham, while enjoying the total silence that surrounded him in his Bentley.

That evening, Beryl's Dad took Jamie to all of the local viewing spots, telling him to be on the lookout for the Home Guard, if they caught him with binoculars they might confiscate them, after all there was a war going on.

After dark, Jamie walked along the cliffs, trying out all of the best spots, finally selecting one that had a complete view of the channel, and he could clearly see the occasional lights coming from the ships travelling both ways through the Channel. He watched until late, but finally had to go back to the Baker's as his eyelids kept closing, he really needed to sleep.

Al, woke him early and insisted that they go for a swim, the sun was shining and the water looked inviting.

The Channel water is cold, always, and only the brave can stay in it for long. Jamie was in and out quickly, and he hurried back to the house for breakfast and a warm up. He asked Reg Baker where the fishing boats were kept.

"I'll take you there Jamie, I'm going fishing with some pals, would you like to come?"

"Oh, yes Mr Baker, I've never been in a proper fishing boat before."

"Mrs B is Packing some lunch, so we can go as soon as she's done."

Al and Beryl had hurried back down to the water, also taking a cut lunch, they planned to take a long walk by themselves to get away from Jamie for a while.

Sitting at the dinner table that evening, having just finished an enjoyable fish dinner. Jamie asked Al. "Did you and Beryl enjoy your promenade along the Pier today?"

"Were you spying on us with those binoculars Jamie?"

Mr Baker interjected with, "No Al, Jamie was with me in a fishing boat, we were catching the fish that you had for dinner today, we both saw you two on the Pier, as our boat went by."

"Sorry Jamie, but you do always seem to know where we are."

"Actually Al, I was very busy catching a fish when we went past the Pier, but Mr Baker drew my attention to you two."

"So where's your fish?"

"I threw it back, because it was too small."

"Just like you, shrimp!"

Jamie ignored the remark and excused himself from the table, he hurried off to his observation post.

He checked every boat, hoping to catch something wrong or different with them, but all appeared to be OK.

He watched a squadron of German bombers fly over towards London, and thought of his Mother, alone in their home. He got a bit teary and decided to go back to the Bakers for company, he started to gather his stuff, when he noticed a light flashing in the distance close to the French coast.

He stopped packing up, and tried to decipher the Morse code message, he didn't recognise it. It wasn't in English, he had copied it down in his notebook and was now in a hurry to give it to Mr Baker to translate, because Beryl had told them that her Dad had been a King's Scout when he was younger.

He found his host in the garden shed, he was by himself, so Jamie was happy to talk to him about his little secret without being ridiculed by Al.

"I can't decipher this Jamie, but I will ask Todd Ellis, the local Home Guard Sergeant to look at it, I'll drop it off at his place tomorrow on the way home." Baker reassured him. And added. "Now, you get some sleep and try to forget tonight's adventures."

Jamie replied with. "Thank you Mr Baker, I will keep it a secret until we know what it was about, probably a boyfriend on a boat sending a message to his girlfriend."

The holiday makers loaded up the car and drove away from the House on the Cliff, stopping outside Todd Ellis's house, where Baker left Jamie's notebook, then proceeded on to Etchingham.

Both Reg Baker and Jamie were both silent on the road home, Al, wondered why his little brother did not speak at all on the way home.

As they lay in bed that night, Al asked him. "Are you sick Jamie?"

"No Al, leave me alone, I'm tired and we have school tomorrow."

Al, wasn't going to accept his excuse and insisted. "You and Mr Baker talk incessantly all the time, but not one word tonight. Why?"

"I can't say Al, you have to trust me please, I will tell you about it when I can." Al realised that it must be important if Mr Baker was involved, so he acquiesced to Jamie's wishes and told him."If you are on another mission, please be careful Jamie, I'll keep silent for now, but I'm watching you closely, you can't dabble with Jerry and get away with it."

After a few moments, Al added. "By the way little Bro, Beryl wants to introduce you to her cousin, she said that you need a girlfriend to take your mind off the war."

Jamie sat bolt upright and shouted. "No she is not, I don't want one, I'm not going to talk to any ugly girls, I'm not getting married, I'll be just like the Colonel, stay single and boss everybody."

The little fellow was angry now and couldn't sleep. He asked himself. "Why don't they leave me alone, a girl will just get in my way, and they're boring."

The following morning at school, Beryl told Jamie that her dad had asked for him to go down to Hastings on Friday again, to meet Todd Ellis.

"Yes Beryl, he might have some information for me, I suppose Al will be coming too?"

"Of course Jamie, he's my boyfriend, you need a friend too."

"No I don't Beryl, I'm a bachelor, just like the Lone Ranger, and that cousin of yours, Fat Gwen, has Acne and she talks funny, so don't bother bringing her down at the weekend."

Beryl just giggled and ran off to find Al.


Friday night and the Bentley pulled up outside the Baker's holiday home, the boys hopped out and Colonel Robertson waved good bye, and drove away happy to be alone in his car, after listening to the constant banter between the brothers.

Jamie walked to the front door and came to a halt as Beryl was standing at the door, she was expecting Al to be first, she turned to a young girl who was standing behind her, she gently pulled her to the front and said. "This is Jamie, Jamie this is my cousin Rachel."

Jamie's stomach hit the ground, he stood motionless as Rachel held out her hand to him, he limply held it, and mumbled something inaudible. Al, pushed him aside and greeted Beryl and her cousin, with a peck on the cheek for both of them.

Jamie's legs were now like jelly, and he desperately wanted to disappear through the floorboards.

Mrs Baker called from the kitchen door. "Why don't you and Rachel sit on the couch while we prepare dinner?" He just sat and watched as Al and Beryl vanished through the kitchen door.

He blurted out. "I have to see if I have my binoculars with me."

Rachel replied. "I can see them poking out of the bag on your shoulder, Jamie."she cooed and smiled at him.

Now he was feeling light headed, he slid sideways off the couch and headed for the kitchen, calling out. "Where is Mr Baker Ma'am?"

"He's down at Todd Ellis's house Jamie, perhaps you and Rachel could go and call him home for dinner." shouted Beryl.

"I'm not sure where he lives Beryl."

Rachel cooed. "I do, we called into Mister Ellis on the way here."

Jamie floated towards the front door and meekly followed Rachel down the road towards The Ellis house.

Todd welcomed them, he already knew Rachel from previous visits, he said. "You're Jamie the detective, right?"

Jamie replied meekly. "Not a detective, Mr Ellis, just a schoolboy sir."

"But Rachel's boyfriend no doubt?

Jamie gulped and then mumbled. "Nooo." Then he turned a bright Red. Reg Baker quickly came to Jamie's aid, saying. "You take Jamie into your office Todd and I'll walk Rachel home for dinner."

Todd explained to Jamie that the Morse messages where in German and he had handed them over to his superior officer, and had been told to forget everything that he knew about them.

He told Jamie. "You must stop observing at night and forget about the whole thing."

Jamie replied. "I'll do that Mr Ellis, in fact I'm a bit scared about it."

"That's normal Jamie, you go home to the Bakers and enjoy the weekend with your new girl."

He shook his head then trudged slowly back to the Bakers, he had decided that he would miss being embarrassed at dinner and go for a long walk on the beach until bed time.

He eventually crept into the house and up to the bedroom that he shared with Al, who was awake and waiting for him. "Enjoy your walk little brother? Did you think about Rachel all of the time?"

"Don't Al, I probably wont sleep tonight."

"She told Beryl that she likes you, and by the way, her Mum is moving them to Etchingham next month, so she will be going to our school."

"Nooo! there goes my schoolwork, I bet she will be in my class, and the only empty desk is in the aisle right next to mine."

Al tried to calm him down with. "We are going to the beach tomorrow for a swim."

Jamie quickly replied. "I don't have any bathers Al, I can't swim in my undies."

"Rachel won't be impressed by that, you have to try harder shrimp."

"Al, don't call me shrimp, or I'll tell Beryl about all of your other girlfriends."

"It's OK buddy, I have two pair of bathers so you can use one, now we need to sleep."

The following day Jamie joined them on the beach, he tried to avoid staring at Rachel but she caught him several times, when that happened he blushed and tried to make an excuse, chattering on about nothing in general.

When it was time to swim, Rachel and Beryl took their jackets off and stood up ready to go in the water.

Jamie just sat with his trousers still on, looking painfully down the beach, he couldn't look at the girl, it made him light headed, and he was feeling very uncomfortable.

Rachel eventually walked up to him and started to pull him up by the arms. He groaned, then said. "I'm feeling really sick guys, I think I'll go back up to the house."

Al shouted at him. "Jamie, don't be such a sook, the girls want to swim, so we will go in with them, now take your trousers off and follow us into the water."

He did as his brother told him, he relaxed a little and started to enjoy himself in the water.

After the swim, on the way back up to the Baker's house, Rachel walked up to his side and slipped her hand into his, he thought about removing it, but realised that it was a very pleasant feeling, so he just kept walking along. He was trying very hard to be nonchalant, and Al and Beryl who were walking behind them, where giggling quietly.

Two weeks later, Jamie was studiously reading his English book in class, when the door opened to reveal the school Principal with Rachel Widmark in tow.

Jamie sat open mouthed while his classmates greeted her as one, she then walked towards the empty desk, as she passed him he glanced sideways at her and she smiled at him, he froze, then turned his head to his book, and pretended to read, he was afraid that his classmates might be aware of the fact that they knew each other, he was now blood red, and was perspiring profusely.

Lunch time arrived, and Jamie quickly grabbed his lunchbox and slid into the aisle, intending to hurry to the playground ahead of the rest, only to be blocked by Rachel, who smilingly took his hand and led him out of the classroom. He followed meekly, unable to resist. Thinking to himself. "What is wrong with me, I must have the Flu or something!"

As they approached the shed where the seating was, she turned to him and whispered. "Shall we sit over there in the sun while we have lunch?"

She was inches away from his face, he caught the sweet perfume of her breath. He immediately thought to himself. "Did I brush my teeth this morning, Oh, yes, after breakfast." Relieved, he answered her. "I'm happy, where ever you want."

She smiled at him, he couldn't take his eyes off her face, holding his hand she led him past the other students, he just followed her to the seat that she had chosen, and meekly sat, almost next to her, leaving a respectful few inches between them.

She turned to him, smiling. "Jamie it's OK, I wont bite you."

He didn't reply, he was mesmerised by her incredibly beautiful big Brown eyes.

After lunch, Jamie sat at his desk, pretending to do his Maths paper, but in fact he was recalling every word that had passed between him and Rachel at lunch time, including all of the questions put to him by almost every boy in his class regarding his relationship with the new girl, everyone asked him if she was his girlfriend and he just shook his head, each time he did, Rachel just smiled.

After school, Al and Beryl met them and the four of them took the bus to the Golf Club, where The Colonel had arranged a game of Golf followed by a dinner with the girls Mothers.

Both of the girls were good at sport, and golf was just another one that they excelled at, Jamie struggled to keep up with them and Al constantly criticised him, but he was happy to be in the company of them all, and he put up with the jibes.

✧ ✧ ✧

# CHAPTER 7

At the Lodge, The Colonel was complaining about the club finances to Betty. The boys were in the next room playing chess, when they heard her say. "Oh, no Colonel who could be taking it?"

They both cocked their ears to listen in, as he replied. "I have no idea Betty, I'm no book keeper, and I don't want to arouse anyone at the club, the word will get around and the culprit will go quiet or disappear entirely."

Betty chipped in with. "Young Al is very good with figures sir, he's getting extra tuition in Accounting at school, he could look at the books for you."

The Colonel then bellowed. "Al, come here lad, I need your help in finding a thief."

"Yes sir, what can I do to help?"

"I want you to examine the Golf Club books, there seems to be an anomaly somewhere, money is going missing."

"But the Treasurer has the books sir, when can I see them?"

"Collins the Treasurer is going into hospital next week for minor surgery, he will hand over the books to me."

Al asked. "Wont the culprit be suspicious sir?"

He replied. "No Al, everyone knows that I hate Book keeping and accounting, they will feel secure, knowing that I wont even look at them while Collins is away."

The following week, Jamie was showing Rachel and Beryl the Mink Farm, teaching them how to handle the animals, without being bitten.

Al was pouring over the Club finances, looking for a fault. He asked the Colonel. "Who handles the cash, sir?"

He replied. "Several people, including, Brett, the shop keeper, Olly the barman and Cathy the waitress."

"Is there a safe on the premises?"

"Yes, it's in the Office."

Al told him. "Well, the books balance, Sir."

"I had already eliminated Collins, he is as honest as the day is long Al."

Al then said. "The missing cash never gets to the Treasurer, but it may get to the safe, if it does, then we can catch the thief red handed, but we will need to have someone watching all the staff that handle cash."

The Colonel asked Al. "Who do you suggest then Al, I can't think of anyone from the club."

"Young Rachel sir, she is really smart and not many club members know her."

"Yes Al, Jamie and Beryl can help her as well, they are always pottering about at the club rooms, so no one will be suspicious of them, run and get them in from the Farm and we will brief them now."

Within a short time the Trap was set, all of the foursome were delighted to be given the task of catching the thief.

Rachel soon had the Club Members eating out of her hands, while she assisted both the Barman Olly, and the Waitress Cathy in their duties, although she sensed a dislike towards her by Cathy, who rarely smiled and gave her the menial tasks to do while she herself socialised with the members, who were always generous with the tips.

Jamie helped Brett in the shop, but made sure not to handle any cash, because he must be above suspicion.

On the following Saturday night, after a Club Dinner dance, most of the members had gone home, leaving The Colonel and his staff to clean up. Everyone was working, Jamie and Brett were stacking the outside furniture up against the rear wall, under the verandah. When they had finished, Brett said his goodbyes and rode off on his motorbike.

Jamie continued to wander round the area looking for any rubbish or maybe a glass or two left outside, he made a last circuit passing the back of the clubhouse, as he walked below a window he thought that he had seen a flash of light. He waited silently, yes there it was again, he then strolled to the end of the building and climbing the verandah, hid behind the rack that normally held the members Clubs.

A familiar voice whispered in his ear. "What are you watching Bro." Jamie whispered back. "Keep your eye on the tractor shed."

Just then a hooded figure appeared from that spot and crept towards the window that Jamie had seen the light flashing from.

They waited until the person climbed into the obviously unlocked window. Jamie told his brother. "You wait for him to climb out, I'll go and tell the Colonel to go into the Office, because that is where that person is and probably now is emptying the unlocked safe."

Both boys went into action quickly, Al stood under the window, waiting for the thief to exit, he intended to wait until his head and shoulders appeared, then he would push him back into the arms of the Colonel and the others.

Jamie had found the Colonel talking to Olly outside the Office, he whispered in his ear, exuding a Bellow from him. "Olly, follow me." with that he marched into the Office just in time to see a pair of legs starting to disappear out of the window, before he could grab them, the person let out a squeal, and was propelled right back into the room, landing on the floor, flat on his back. Both Olly and the Colonel fell on him. Then Al's smiling face appeared at the window. "Did you catch him Sir? By the way, he dropped this." Chuckling as he tossed a bag full of cash onto the floor next to the felon.

"Bloody wonderful Al, perfect timing."

Jamie entered, accompanied by Beryl, Rachel and a very unhappy Cathy, who was resisting and trying to get out of the grip of the young girls.

"Here's your other culprit Colonel." He cried.

Beryl shouted out "She and Brett are partners unbeknown to you Sir, she opened the Safe and the back window, then sent him a signal with the torch."

Rachel chimed in with. "Jamie picked up on the flashlight and waited with Al for Brett to appear."

The Colonel told Olly to ring the Police, and he bound both the thieves hands and sat them on the floor to await the local constabulary.

After the Police Officers had taken all of the statements and evidence including the two offenders off to the Station, The Colonel opened the bar for him and Olly also soft drinks for the young detectives.

Having now managed to get rid of the people responsible for the vanishing money, both boys had to fill in at the Golf Shop after school and at weekends, and both girls shared the waitressing duties as well, that had been fun for a couple of weeks but now they were wanting to return to Hastings for their weekends.

Thankfully, the Colonel had found a willing young man to run the Shop, and one of the members daughters was to start waiting on tables.

# CHAPTER 8

Back on the beach at Hastings again, the four were playing cricket, as young English youths do, except for Jamie, who kept looking out to sea.

Rachel called out to him. "What's so interesting out there Jamie? you seem mesmerised by the ships passing by,"

He looked at her and said. "I'm not happy about the signals that I saw, I know that I'm not supposed to talk about it, but I can't stop thinking that something is wrong."

That, seemed to make them all a bit glum, so they walked home slowly and talked amongst themselves about the signals."

After dinner, Rachel and Jamie went for a walk along the cliff top, just as the sun was setting, She tried to cheer him up but he once again looked out to sea every few seconds.

After sunset, as they were finally walking home, Rachel stopped in her tracks, grabbed Jamie's arm and whispered. "Look, it's a light flashing out there."

"Rachel, you call out the dots and dashes and I'll write them down in my notebook"

She did as he asked, and they monitored the messaging for some time, when it stopped, they hurried home and Jamie told her. "Not a word to anyone, your Uncle will only be cross with me, when I get back to the Mansion I'm going to talk to the Colonel about it, and I'll do whatever he tells me to, then I'll tell you, because you are my assistant now."

Rachel smiled at him, kissed him softly on his cheek, and whispered. "Thank you boss!"

The journey home was carried out in virtual silence, Mrs Baker had put it down to the Foursome being tired. Al sensed that something was wrong again, as Jamie and Rachel usually chatted like a couple of Pigeons, but tonight they just huddled in the corner of the back seat in complete silence, so he decided to wait until he and Jamie were alone, then he would grill his little brother.

Mr Baker dropped the boys off at the Manor, and they said their goodbyes. Al was no sooner in the front door, when he started his questions.

Jamie refused to answer, and told him to come with him to the Colonels office. The Colonel welcomed them both back home and enquired as to their weekend away.

Jamie spoke up immediately. "Sir, I have something to tell you and Al."

"Sounds important young man. Out with it then."

Jamie placed his new notebook on the desk in front of his Host. "Please don't be angry Sir, I thought that I was doing the right thing, but Mr Ellis's boss shut us down, so I decided to ask your opinion about these messages, they might only be some sailor letting his girlfriend know how he was, but I just can't help being suspicious."

The Colonel looked long and hard at the boy, he knew that Jamie was a smart lad and he was going to give him the benefit of the doubt, by reading the notebook.

"Sit down boys and relax, while I study the notes."

Al looked at Jamie questioningly, he said nothing, as he did not want to distract the Colonel, who was reading with a furrowed brow.

After some minutes, he put the notebook aside and asked. "Who else knows about this?"

Jamie quickly listed all of the people that knew that he was watching from the clifftop.

"I want both of you to contact your girlfriends straight away, and tell them that they must not say a word to anyone about this matter, you can use the telephone in the hall to do that, now go and leave me to make some calls from the office phone."

"Yes sir." Echoed both boys as they left the room.

Al held Jamie's arm and whispered. "It must be very serious Bro, I've never seen him like this before."

Jamie replied. "Yes, you're right, you go first on the phone because I'll be a while, I have something else to tell Rachel as well."

Al smiled as he started to dial the Baker's number.

Although Colonel Robertson had been placed on the Reserve list some years before, he had a magnificent army record, and was well known to several high ranking Officers, both in the Army and Navy, he had in fact Hosted Sir Winston Churchill on one occasion. He was now making use of these contacts in getting the Morse message to the right people in a hurry.

In the morning at breakfast he told the boys that he had spoken to Todd Ellis and Reg Baker, and they and their wives had also been sworn to secrecy.

"You lads just try to carry on as usual with the Girls and their parents, we don't want anyone getting a smell of this yet."

Jamie replied. "Yes sir, are you going to keep my notebook?" "Absolutely," Roared the Colonel. "I'm getting it framed." Jamie smiled weakly and croaked. "Really sir?"

"Only bloody joking little man, let's all just relax a little and see what comes of this."

Betty Lawton poked her head around the door and said. "That language is a bit rich for a small boy sir."

"Sorry Betty, I thought you were in the Kitchen, but no you were spying on us males."

With that they all broke into laughter, with Betty pretending to be annoyed and huffily departing.

Keeping secrets can be very hard for most people, and it's extremely hard for young adults. The Foursome were at least able to whisper amongst themselves when out of earshot of other students, they spent a lot of time on the Golf course and helping the two new employees out when they could.

Beryl had told them that they wouldn't be going back down to Hastings anytime soon, as her Dad had been asked to keep the family away for a while. Jamie concluded that it had something to do with the Morse signals. He told them that he might have been spotted the last time on the cliff.

Al said. "Jamie they may have a hit out on you, you might be better off wearing a disguise."

"Don't be stupid Al, Jerry has got bigger fish to fry than me."

Beryl chimed in with. "Maybe Adolf Hitler found out who caught his spy in Dorset and he's coming after you."

"That one officially went down to Mr Bullymore, so I'm in the clear."

They continued teasing Jamie all the way around the Golf course, and into the Clubhouse.

That evening they all had dinner at the Clubhouse with the Colonel, later he dropped the girls off at their homes and then drove out of Etchingham, towards Tunbridge Wells. The boys ignored the fact that The Colonel had failed to inform them where they were going, after all he was a very important and busy man, so they just went along with whatever he did and enjoyed the ride in the comfort of the Bentley.

Several miles out of Tunbridge, he pulled the car into a siding and switched off the motor,

Jamie couldn't help himself, He asked the Colonel. "Sir, what are we doing here, is it to do with the Morse messages."

"Try to relax for a while Boys, all will be revealed to you as soon as I can." This comforted the boys for a while and they even started to play Rock, Paper and Scissors, until they disagreed on that.

Just as both boys were becoming totally bored, an Armoured vehicle pulled up beside them. The Colonel left the Bentley and entered the ARV. He spent some ten minutes inside, then climbed back into the Bentley, smiling.

He waited until the ARV had left, then turned to the boys and told them that following observations by certain concerned citizens, a German Submarine had been sunk just off the coast near Hastings.

The journey home was now happy and both the Colonel and Al heaped praise on Jamie. The Colonel told the boys that the Person in the RV was a very high ranking Naval Officer, and that they must forget about the evenings meeting.

The following morning, the boys met both girls in the School Hall, where Rachel was pinning a picture taken from the daily paper, of a German submarine, beached, near Hastings, with a hole in the hull.

He asked her. "What's this Rachel?"

"Oh, you don't know Master Jamie Dexter?"

"Rachel, You know as much as I do, we are a team at golf and just about everything else, you should also be proud of the picture."

Beryl told the couple to stand under the picture together, as she wanted to take a photo of them, then added. "By the way guys, we are all welcomed back to Hastings, so I hope that you can join us this Friday evening.

Rachel and Jamie looked at each other and grinned.

Beryl saw them looking like two Cheshire cats, saying. "You two sit next to each other in class everyday, you are always together at the Club, now because you can spend another weekend in each others company, you act like it's Christmas, boy Jamie and you didn't want a girlfriend last month."

He stated. "Beryl, Rachel and I are still not technically boyfriend and girlfriend, but she has agreed to be my assistant, when we are investigating anything."

"Rachel, is that true?"

"Just the part about the assistant detective. And by the way, you and Al spend just as much time with each other as we do."

"But we admit we're a couple, Rachel, you two are in denial."
"I'm not, but he is, he thinks we're just buddies."

Jamie shouted, "Hello, I'm still here, you two, it's just that I don't want Al telling everybody that I have a girl, he makes fun of me all the time."

Beryl took his hand and looking into his eyes, said. "I'll tell Al that you are just buddies, if you admit that you are nuts about my cousin, OK?"

He looked at Rachel and sheepishly agreed.

Once again she smiled at him, took his other hand a kissed him on his cheek again.

❖ ❖ ❖

# CHAPTER 9

David, the new Club Shop Manager, was the first to arrive in the morning, as he was riding his motorbike through the gate on the way to the clubhouse, he spotted something protruding out of the Bunker near the seventeenth hole. He rode across the fairway towards the object, to get a better look. He stopped dead in his tracks when he saw the tail end of a massive bomb sticking up out of the sand trap.

He'd only recently been discharged from the Air Force, after an accident which badly damaged his leg, he was used to seeing bombs, as he had loaded them into the RAF Bombers. He realised that this one would be unexploded. He headed straight for the shop, unlocked the door and dialled the Police. Having informed them of the Bomb he then rang the Colonel.

Jamie was sitting in the Bentley, still rubbing sleep from his eyes when he asked The Colonel. "What's so important Sir? I was sound asleep when you dragged me out of bed."

Al replied for the Colonel. "David found an unexploded bomb in a bunker at the Golf club, there was an air raid on London last night and a Jerry plane must have unloaded its bombs after turning back home, one fell on Tunbridge Wells and caused a lot of damage and it looks like one decided to fall in our bunker."

Meanwhile they had arrived at the Golf Club, and parked a long way away from the Bunker in question, no harm must come to the Colonels pride and joy, his Motor car.

Several Policemen were erecting temporary barriers to close off the danger zone.

A Chief Inspector, told the Colonel that the Bomb squad was on it's way and the public were now prohibited from entering the Golf Club grounds and the surrounding area.

The boys were busy making tea and coffee for the official workers, and also cooking breakfast for themselves and the Colonel, they were told to remain in the Clubhouse until the bomb had been removed.

An Army Major accompanied by two warrant Officers arrived in a Jeep, they went straight to the bomb, took a cursory look, the senior officer left the two bomb experts alone with the missile. He then directed everybody to retire behind the Clubhouse.

The silence was frightening, everyone was half expecting a huge explosion, but praying for none, the two brave bomb disposal lads were handling the huge monster very gently, then a shout came from the bunker. "All clear sir, we can now lift it out when the crane arrives."

Everyone started talking at once, the relief from the tension was obvious, The Major went to his jeep and using his wireless ordered the crane crew to enter through the wooded area next to the bunker, he had previously arranged this point of entry with the Colonel, it would mean that they had to dismantle the wire fence surrounding the course, but only enough to allow the mobile crane through. Although the bomb was unarmed it was still loaded with explosive material, and it would have to be transported to a secure area by road, escorted by Military Police, then dismantled safely.

The boys watched as the crane lumbered through the woods and the crew secured the huge bomb to it, pulled it free from the sand bunker and carrying it back through the woods to the waiting truck and escort.

David and the two boys took shovels and worked on repairing the damaged bunker.

The usual early morning golfers had started to turn up, after having been stopped on the road, while the bomb squad was working. Great excitement circulated around the course, while the boys told the members what had taken place. After some time normality returned and Golf replaced all of the chatter.

Later that day, the girls arrived from school and the whole story was repeated to them.

"So, you two were cooking eggs, and stuffing yourselves while those two brave soldiers risked there lives, is that what you are saying?" asked Beryl.

Al quickly replied with. "We had to replace the sand in the bunker too."

"Yes, after the bomb was twenty miles up the road." quipped Rachel.

Jamie crooned.

"You girls have no idea how we both cheated death this morning."

Both girls burst into laughter, and hardly stopped giggling the whole way round the eighteen holes.

# CHAPTER 10

The following Thursday evening, Jamie and Rachel were playing a late nine holes together, Al and Beryl were studying for an exam for the following morning.

At that time of the year in wartime, England had double daylight saving, that is an extra two hours of daylight each night, at the height of summer it only got dark at ten o'clock at night, allowing them to play until late.

Jamie having won the last hole, had teed off first, slicing his shot away to the right, and into the long grass down the side of the fairway, he waited for Rachel to hit, She managed to hook her shot, and it sailed off into the trees on the left hand side by the seventeenth bunker. He wandered off to find his ball and she went in the opposite direction, to search among the trees.

He took a while to find his ball then he chipped back on to the fairway, leaving his clubs next to the ball, he took a five iron out and set off to help Rachel, who appeared to be having trouble finding hers, he shouted to her. "Just drop another ball, Rachel, we're not playing for sheep stations."

There was no reply so he called again. "Rachel, give it up, drop another ball, you are four shots better than me anyway." Still no reply, he walked deeper into the wooded area, calling out, then he tripped up on a club, it was her chipper, with the red leather handle, the same as all of her clubs. Then he called out in alarm. "Rachel, where are you, are you hurt?" He was now panicking, he ran towards the boundary fence, looking every which way for his young friend, calling her name all the time. He had now reached the fence, right where they had dismantled it to let the crane in. He looked around and saw her Red Golf glove laying on the side of the road.

Dave had heard Jamie calling and realised that there was something wrong, he called out to Olly, then told him that he was going to find the young ones. He didn't let his bad leg stop him scurrying into the Copse, calling out as he went, he arrived at the boundary fence, and saw Jamie lying on the road holding Rachel's glove and sobbing loudly.

He picked the boy up and walked him back to the Clubhouse, assuring him that everything would be all right.

The Clubhouse virtually shook as the Colonel barked orders and shouted angrily. "Why the hell would anyone abduct a young girl from a golf course, how did they know she was playing at this time? What the hell is going on?"

No one was game to offer an answer.

The local police Inspector had arrived, and had the area sealed off. Rachel's Mother Dulcie had been informed of her daughter's absence, and she had hurried to the Club.

Jamie had now recovered a little from the shock and told the Colonel "Rachel has never spoken about her Dad, shouldn't we let him know, is he still alive Sir?"

"She won't talk about him, because he has an important job in the Admiralty." Then he stopped in his tracks. "Bloody hell of course, it will be about the Convoys." He ran to the phone and quickly dialled the Admiralty number. Then barking into the phone. "I need to speak to Admiral Sharp, urgently."

Commander Eric Widmarks job was to control the management of the Convoys out of Canada and the US. He would organise the Royal Navy escort ships to meet the convoys somewhere of the American coast, then keep them safe from German submarines on the way to England.

He had just left Admiralty house on the way to catch his ride home, he was going to meet his colleague, Lieutenant Commander Hawkins in his car at the end of Westminster Bridge, he was enjoying a brisk walk across the Bridge, but was a little inconvenienced by the thick fog drifting up from the Thames, when a black vehicle pulled up beside him, two men jumped out of the car, one pushed him towards the vehicle, while the other hit him on the head with a heavy rubber cosh, he collapsed and was quickly loaded into the back seat, the car then took off at speed across the bridge towards the South of London.

Hawkins, was sitting in his car facing in the direction that the Commander would be coming from, he had vaguely seen the fracas near the Big Ben side of the Bridge, he thought that he had recognised the Commander's Uniform through the fog, but was not quite sure, so he watched as the car passed him, he got a quick look inside the back window and saw a flash of the three gold bands on Widmarks arm, who had obviously pushed his arm against the window hoping that someone would see it, he must have recovered from the blow on the head, there could only be one Naval Commander on that Bridge that night.

Hawkins was parked on the wrong side of the road, he managed to do a U turn with great difficulty, then started to follow the car in question, but he soon lost it in the traffic and the Fog.

The Colonel had now assumed that Rachel would be used as a lever to get her Father to inform Jerry of the Convoys movements.

He was on the phone to the Admiral once again, when he finally got off the phone he sadly informed the small group that Rachel's dad had also disappeared.

He had been abducted, and it had been witnessed by a Naval Officer, one of his Colleagues, who chased the car but lost it, then he informed the Admiral of the make and colour of the car, plus part of the Registration number.

The Police Inspector told the Colonel that a local farmer had seen a black Austin driving away at speed towards London around the time of Rachel's abduction, the pieces of the puzzle were now falling into place, as the Commander would probably be held in the City, with his daughter.

The Colonel closed the Clubhouse and shop and asked Olly and David if they would help him in finding the girl, both immediately agreed and they climbed into the Bentley, along with Jamie and drove to the Mansion to pick up Al.

The Colonel ran into his office and came back with Al, a large Handgun and a box of ammunition, they then headed off towards the London road.

Olly knew that the Colonel was an accurate shot during his time in the Army. He had dozens of trophies as well as animal Pelts in his Great room to prove it.

They drove straight to the Dexter home in Greenwich, where Di and Ted were waiting for them. Ted greeted his two sons and then was introduced to Olly and Dave, he told the Colonel that he had taken leave immediately on hearing about the abduction, he knew he would have to be near his boys at this time. Robertson asked him if he had his sidearm with him. He answered. "Yes Sir, at all times during war."

Di organised a late meal for them, and they gathered in the lounge room to discuss tactics.

Ted Dexter suggested that they split up into two groups, the first led by The Colonel, with Olly and Al to assist. The second consisting of himself, Dave and Jamie.

All agreed to this and The Colonel said that he would concentrate on Commander Widmark, while Ted and his crew would look for Rachel, this suited Jamie as he was finding it hard to think of anything but his girl.

Dexter's jeep, was equipped with a radio, and he had friends in the Metropolitan Police who were also happy to help him. It wasn't long before he got a tip that the Austin had been spotted by a PC Johnson in Deptford and it was now under surveillance by that officer. Dexter's little group mounted the jeep and sped off towards the river suburb, where they found PC Johnson in a concealed doorway, he quickly pointed out the suspect house where the Austin was parked.

Dave and Jamie commenced their investigation of the car, they had spotted a man slumped in the drivers seat, his head was resting on the steering wheel, he was either asleep, dead or drugged.

Jamie climbed the side fence and was looking in the lower windows of the house, keeping below the window ledges, and listening for any sounds from within.

Dave had now asserted that the driver of the car was in fact asleep, as he was breathing shallowly. Not wanting to waken him, but needing to signal to Ted Dexter the fact that there was someone in the car, he waved his hands in Ted's direction and emitted a low whistle. Ted looked over at him and decided to slowly approach the car.

Meanwhile PC Johnson remained in his position ready to warn any arriving Officers of the teams whereabouts.

Jamie had completed a circuit of the house and was about to go to his dad and report, when he saw a flash of light appear from the very top window, but it had just as quickly disappeared, nevertheless he has seen a light and he figured that it was from a torch being quickly switched on and off. He continued to watch. After several seconds it flashed again.

He sidled up to his Dad and whispered. "There's a flashlight being turned on and off in the upstairs room, it may be a Morse signal, I'll continue to watch and try to read it."

Dexter told his son. "It could be Rachel trying to attract attention, she seems to be a smart young lass, yes Jamie, keep watching and I will keep my eye on you as well."

Back at the Embankment, beside the River Thames, Colonel Robertson was watching a Motor boat easing towards the shore, he thought it suspicious as it was not showing any navigation lights, which was a serious offence on the river at night. He told Olly. "You keep watching Olly while Al and I creep up for a closer look."

As they approached a figure came onto the boat deck and threw a rope onto the shore, where to their total surprise a man grabbed the rope and tied it up to the metal railing. Both Al and the Colonel froze, waiting for the next move from the boats crew.

The mystery figure had boarded the boat and both men went below deck.

The Colonel and Al crawled along the retaining wall to get even closer, then a shrill whistle from Olly alerted them of a car approaching along the embankment road towards where the boat was moored. They both crouched low in the shadows and waited.

Outside the house in Deptford, the driver of the car was stirring, he sat upright and lit a cigarette, opened his window and looked towards the front door of the house.

Jamie was now perched directly under the window where the torch light had come from, again it flashed, this time the driver of the car had seen it, he quickly stubbed out his fag, barged out of the car and started to run to the front door, only to be stopped by Dave diving at his ankles and pulling him down in a Rugby tackle.

Dexter was quickly upon him, kneeling on his neck, which prevented him from calling out, then he whipped off the man's belt and tied his hands and feet together, stuffing his tie in his mouth as a gag. He questioned him about his reason for being there. The man mumbled in German, Dexter took the tie out of his mouth, held him by the throat then asked again, this time he mumbled a well known swear word in German, Dexter stuffed the tie back in and pushed it down, nearly choking him, then he and Dave threw him unceremoniously onto the backseat of the car, and locked the doors.

At the Embankment, the motor car pulled up next to where the boat was moored.

Olly had spotted a Policeman standing near the Police box a couple of hundred feet further down the Embankment road, he moved as quickly and silently as he could, reliving his Army days under the Colonel in India.

He told the PC about the Motor boat with no lights and behaving suspiciously, also that he suspected that both it and the car were involved in the Abduction of Commander Widmark and his daughter. The Officer used the telephone inside the Police box and rang the River Police and informed them of the situation.

As the car had pulled up, a man left the boat and stepped ashore, and spoke to the people in the car, then two men got out of the car and started to drag what looked like a body out of the boot.

The Colonel and Al waited until the whole of the body appeared, and quickly recognising the uniform of a Naval Officer, they both said. "It's the Commander."

The Colonel, Handgun at the ready, ran to the car shouting out in his booming voice. "You are all under arrest, Hands high in the air now."

The man from the boat ignoring the Colonel, drew a pistol, he hadn't even had a chance to direct it at anyone, when a thirty eight calibre bullet entered his right thigh, sending him into a screaming heap on the road, his pistol clattered onto the pavement.

The other two men had dropped the Commander and were running towards the boat, The Colonel was now in full chase. Olly had joined the party and had picked up the pistol and was running with his Boss towards the boat, that was slowly pulling away from the dock.

Al hurriedly untied the Commander and helped him to his feet, as the PC arrived and all three ran to the Pier beside Olly and The Colonel.

One of the men had managed to jump onto the boat as it pulled away, the other was calling out for them to come back for him in German. Olly hit him in the back of the neck and he fell onto the Pier, the Ex Sergeant Major then landed heavily on him, making him squeal like a pig.

The Motor boat sped up the River towards Westminster Bridge, just as the River Police boat emerged from around a Pylon, the motor boat lost control and ploughed straight into the Pylon, capsizing it and spilling all of its contents and passengers into the river..

The River Police then began to fish them out, handcuffing them all. Commander Widmark and the PC interrogated the wounded German and he spilled the beans very quickly, he had no liking for the pain inflicted on him by Rachel's Father. He told them of the address in Deptford immediately.

Leaving the Germans from the car and boat with the Metropolitan Police, the team was now increased to four by Commander Widmark, they all climbed into the Bentley and raced to Deptford to help find Rachel.

Outside the house in Deptford, Captain Dexter and David were discussing how best to break into the house, Ted had been waiting for a Police officer to arrive, with the authority to arrest, but was now contemplating going ahead without them. He signalled Jamie to keep watching the house.

Then a shout from Jamie. "Dad, I just saw Rachel at the window, she's struggling with someone, now they have gone and the light's gone out. He's hurting her dad, let's go in please."

With that, Ted and Dave ran towards the front door and with their combined weight, broke into the hallway. Ted drew his weapon and they both advanced towards the stairs, he shouted out. "Come out with your hands up now. Unhand the girl and you wont be harmed."

A man appeared on the balcony above, he was holding Rachel by the hair, and dragging her behind him grinning and shouting in German.

Ted Dexter had a clear view of him and was confident to be able to hit him, without harming Rachel.

The German raised his weapon intending to fire.

Ted fired one round, striking him on his right calf, he shouted an obscenity, then fell down the stairs, releasing Rachel's hair as he collapsed.

Jamie jumped over the injured German and raced up the stairs to the waiting arms of his now happy girlfriend.

Below stairs was a hive of activity, with The Colonel's team arriving also a Police Inspector with his crew in tow. Commander Widmark leapt up the stairs to embrace his young daughter, then thanked Jamie for comforting her, the three were all smiles now and were in a hurry to get to Greenwich to see Mrs Widmark, who had gone to the Dexter house to wait with Di.

After disposing of the necessary statements and Prisoners, the whole group travelled together to Greenwich, where the celebrations took place, late into the night.

Admiral Sharp arrived to join them and to thank everyone for a splendid effort. He also told Rachel, Jamie and Al, that they were welcome to accompany him and Commander Widmark on a visit to Portsmouth in the following week to go aboard one of his battleships. All three were keen to do this and thanked him excitedly.

⟡ ⟡ ⟡

# CHAPTER 11

Rachel's Dad, drove them home from Portsmouth, after spending several hours there, visiting a Submarine, a Destroyer and a huge Battleship, which they were not permitted to know the name of, due to security reasons, The Commander had managed to include Beryl, being Rachel's best girlfriend. All four had a great time, and were treated as VIP's during the visit. Beryl had been so pleased to be included that she was now planning to return the compliment somehow.

She looked at Al and whispered in his ear. "Do you think, Rachel would like to go horse riding on the weekend?"

He quickly answered. "Yes, providing that Jamie and I can come too."

"Of course silly, it wouldn't be half so much fun without you two clowns."

"Do you know someone who has four placid Ponies, Jamie and I are beginners you know."

"Yes, my dad has a Friend who runs a riding school, I can ask him, we can go and ring him now."

It was eight o'clock on the next Saturday morning when the Colonel dropped the foursome off at the Molloy Riding school, Mitch Molloy greeted them and led them to the stables to select their mounts, Beryl and Rachel had been riding horses for years so they picked spirited ponies for themselves, and plodders for the boys.

After saddling up they headed towards the road, led by Beryl, who knew the area well. They walked the horses for a mile or so, to allow them to get used to the riders on their backs. Then Beryl broke her pony into a trot, and the others followed in single file.

They headed towards the coast, and rode up to the edge of the cliffs overlooking the Channel, they dismounted, and let the horses rest while they watched the ships going each way.

The girls had packed food for the day, and they each had a water bottle and a gas mask, just in case.

Beryl suggested that they ride to Battle, where the Battle of Hastings had been held Nine hundred years before, and was actually Seven Miles from Hastings.

Jamie became enthused, he said. "I can search for the arrow that killed King Harold, apparently no one ever claimed it."

Al replied. "That's because there is no proof that he died from an arrow in the eye."

"But the Bayeux Tapestry shows him with an arrow in his eye."

"Actually, Jamie, that wasn't the King, history just say's he died at the Battle."

Jamie was a bit sad about the arrow theory and said. "Well, can we at least have lunch then."

They all agreed to eat lunch and let the horses rest and munch the lush grass.

Jamie continued to go on about Harold's death and the arrow, then told them. "I'm going to see the Tapestry and work it out for myself."

Al laughingly replied. "It's kept in the Bayeux Museum, in Normandy, France Jamie, you'll need Hitler's permission before you can go, and you have no hope after helping to catch his spies."

All three laughed at him and Beryl jibed. "If you go now Hitler will get you."

Having finished lunch, they mounted up and rode away from Battle, toward the Great Woods, a few miles down the road.

The girls had no problem riding through the woods, but both boys were constantly trying to guide their mounts through the trees, until Al realised that the horse would go it's own way regardless, and it was usually the right way.

Beryl was now out of the woods and galloping across a large field to who knows where, Rachel had decided to stop and wait for the boys, at the edge of the woods.

Al emerged from the trees and they both dismounted, to wait for slowcoach Jamie, who had also dismounted and was now leading his limping pony through the trees.

Eventually he too came out of the woods, Al shouted. "Why is your pony limping bro?'

"He's got a stone in his shoe, and I don't have a knife."

Al took out his scout knife and pried the stone out of the shoe, making Jamie's pony a trifle happier.

All three mounted up and followed the track left behind Beryl's pony, but at a much slower pace than her. Riding in single file they arrived at a dead end, it looked like cliff edge. Al dismounted and walked up to the edge, shouting. "It's a Quarry, but where is Beryl?"

They all stood on the edge of the quarry, looking for any sign of Beryl or her pony. Jamie saw a horse emerge from behind a massive pile of sand, he shouted out. "There's her pony, and it looks OK, but where is she?"

Al told the other two to ride into Battle, to use the main road and get help at the Police Station, tell them the name of the Quarry is Simpson Sand and Gravel.

Jamie asked him. "What are you going to do Al? it looks dangerous down there, lots of rocks and earth moving equipment, be careful."

"I'll be OK bro, I'll slide down the side here, it looks pretty safe, and there's a big pile of sand at the bottom, probably where the pony fell."

Jamie and Rachel rode towards the main road, to get help. Al tethered his pony to a tree then sitting on his butt, slipped down the edge of the quarry, hoping for a soft landing.

It had just started to rain heavily and everything soon became wet and the soil quickly turned to mud, which made the going harder for Al. He managed to slide straight into a large puddle and was now soaking wet and cold. He kept calling out to Beryl, but there was no reply.

Rachel and Jamie rode as quickly as they could along the main road, arriving in Battle soaking wet, they found the Police Station, they dismounted and Jamie ran inside, blurting out. "Please help us sir, our friend rode her horse over the edge of the quarry, and we don't know where she is."

The Sergeant asked him. "Which quarry is it son?" Jamie wheezed. "Simpson Sand and Slate, sir."

The Sergeant handed over the desk duties to a constable and led Jamie outside to his Squad car saying. "Tie your nags up to the water trough, and have your girlfriend jump in the car, we'll be at the quarry in a jiffy."

Al was becoming more and more dejected by the soaking rain, and the fact that he couldn't find Beryl. He headed towards a shed near the Sand pile, after turning the corner he stumbled on a leg, falling into the mud once again. This time he was happy, because the leg belonged to Beryl.

She was conscious but very weak, and very wet and cold. He asked her where she was hurt, she whispered to him that her arm was hurting really bad and she couldn't move it. He kicked open the door of the shed and carefully lifted her to her feet and gently lay her on a pile of rags inside, out of the rain, then he opened her rucksack that he had taken from her back and took out her coat, wrapping her up in it, then he made her drink from her water bottle.

The Police car pulled up outside the Quarry gate, The Sergeant jumped out and took a huge pair of bolt cutters out of the boot, using them to snap the lock in half, he opened the gate and drove up to the main office.

Al had heard the car arriving and ran out of the shed shouting out. "We're here in the old shed near the sand pile."

Jamie called out. "Were coming Al, Sergeant Grimes is here to help us."

The Sergeant looked at the young fellow, smiled and said. "No Jamie, you and your girlfriend were the heroes, riding through the storm to get help."

Having now arrived at the shed, he quickly attended to Beryl, first making her comfortable, then he gently felt for any damage, finally deciding that she had probably dislocated her right shoulder, also broken a bone in her arm which he secured to her side, and with the help of the two boys, they loaded her into the car.

He then told Jamie and Rachel to round up the other two Ponies and ride back to Battle and pick up their own mounts, then take them all back to the Riding School.

He and Al got into the car and he quietly told Al to comfort Beryl, as it was going to be a bumpy ride to Hastings Hospital.

The owner of Simpson Sand and Gravel lived in a large house in Battle, Mr Simpson opened his front door and was confronted by two policemen. One officer handed him a summons to appear in court on charges of, failing to provide a safety fence on the edge of his quarry.

Hastings Hospital recovery ward was where Beryl lay, having just awakened from the an aesthetic, following manipulation to put her shoulder back in place and having her forearm reset and put in plaster. She was feeling much more comfortable now, but was not looking forward to the conversation that she was going to have with her parents. She would have to take all of the blame for the accident, as well as apologise to Al, Jamie and Rachel for causing so much trouble for them and spoiling the ride.

The nurse came in and wheeled her bed out, down a passage and into a private room, which the Colonel had paid for. She now waited to face her Parents and her friends.

The Colonel had bought three large bunches of flowers, one each, for the three teenagers.

They burst into Beryl's room grinning like idiots, and waving the flowers, then Rachel gave her a huge hug, followed by Al and Jamie. They refused to let her be guilty for what had happened, as she was in pain and suffering enough from the embarrassment.

When her parents did arrive, they were angry at first, but after talking to the Colonel they decided that Beryl was already being punished, she was going to be incapacitated for quite a while during the weeks ahead.

✧ ✧ ✧

# CHAPTER 12

Captain Ted Dexter was talking on the phone to Colonel Robertson. "So Ted, this mystery vehicle turned up again last night?"

"Yes Sir, I walked over to talk to the driver, but he just started the motor, accelerated and drove quickly away."

"How would you describe the vehicle Ted?"

"It was a delivery type van, shiny black in colour, that's about all I can recall."

"Why would he have been watching your place Ted?"

"It could only be something to do with the abduction Colonel."

"Ted, everyone involved in the abduction is locked up nice and tight, none of our names appear anywhere in the arresting documents, we were all incognito."

"Maybe something else the boys were involved in recently?" "You mean the Mink robbery Ted?"

"Yes sir,"

"Same thing, He is in jail, his mates disowned him, they have no reason to harm anyone."

"Look Ted, just keep an eye open, if he comes back, ring the Police, OK?"

"OK sir, goodbye for now."

The Colonel then spoke to the boys about the mystery van. "Have either of you any idea what this is about?"

Al replied. "No sir, it might just be a coincidence."

"Well let's hope so Al, we've had enough drama this month, just keep you're wits about you as usual, meanwhile I am going to the Regimental Dinner tonight, I'll catch up with Mr Ellicot, and I'll ask him if he might have an idea what this is all about."

The following morning at breakfast, The Colonel told the boys about his talk with Ellicot on the previous night.

"He told me that there had been a strange occurrence there some weeks ago, when a man with an accent was asking about some of his evacuees, he dismissed it, as no one can get access to his boys, they are constantly observed by his three daughters and staff, but he did say that the man drove a Grey van, and he had a big nose."

Al offered. "Maybe he was a sexual deviate sir."

"That's what Ellicot thought as well Al, so he alerted the Police, but the van never came back."

Jamie, who had been silent all this time, spoke up. "The Van that Dad saw was Black, Rector Ellicot's Van was Grey sir, it doesn't make sense."

"You're right Jamie, none of this makes sense, which tells me that we need to be watchful, I'm going to ask Dave at the club to move in here for some added security."

"That's a great idea sir, he can teach me and Jamie unarmed combat."

Jamie quipped. "I use my brain Al, not my body."

Al replied. "Jamie you've had more hidings than any other boy in England."

"No I haven't Al, just that one at the Rectory, and he was just angry."

The Colonel interceded with. "Smart people don't get beaten up Al, Jamie is right, you must use your brains, but I still recommend the unarmed combat lessons for both of you."

Saturday morning, and a Glossy Black Van was travelling along the highway towards Etchingham.

Ex Pastor Williams was singing one of his Welsh hymns, and grinning happily, he was also chatting to himself. "I am so smart, I tricked that silly woman in the Evacuees office, and she gave me the new Billet address for the Dexter boys."

He chuckled again, then said. "I'll get two birds with one stone, and we'll be rid of those vile little creatures for good, I can then continue to roam around England and right all of the wrongs that have happened to my country."

He sang another Welsh hymn, then continued his diatribe against the lads. "Al Dexter dared to abduct my daughter, but I thwarted him and his sneaky little brother, now I will rid the country of them."

He then broke into the Welsh national anthem, and happily continued on his way.

Beryl was back serving in the Bakery, with one arm in plaster and in a sling. The front door flew open and Williams entered, demanding. "Two hot pies girl, and hurry, I'm on a mission."

"Do you want curry or plain, sir?"

"Did I say curry girl?"

"No sir, so it's two plain pies then."

"Oh, my goodness are all children stupid in this country?" "Here are your pies sir."

He threw a ten shilling note on the counter, grabbed the pies and started to shove one in his mouth.

Beryl took advantage of him not being able to talk with half a pie in his mouth, and said."Here's your change sir, and no we are not all stupid, goodbye."

He almost choked on the pie, spluttered something in Welsh, shook his fist at her and walked out.

She watched him stalk to his Black van, and drive off in a hurry.

Jamie and Al sat in the back of the Bentley, while Robertson and Dave rode in the front, they were on the way to the Golf Club to prepare for the Saturday Tournament and the Club dinner dance to follow.

The Colonel gave Jamie a list of food to buy from the Bakery, as he pulled up outside the shop door.

"No idle gossiping now Jamie, we are in a hurry today its going to be full on at the club."

"Yes sir." Jamie said, smiling to himself. "That's why your sending me and not Al, he would have taken all day".

He opened the shop door for a lady to leave, then he entered, walked up to Beryl and gave her the list, with a twinkle in his eye.

She looked at him, took the list, and strode off to fill it, she knew that Al was still in the car, and she knew why.

She returned quickly with his filled order, handing it to him saying. "Ask the Colonel, was that quick enough?"

Jamie replied. "Sorry Beryl, it's not my idea."

"It's not your idea, I know, I was already upset by a mad foreigner earlier today."

"What happened?"

"He was a pig, he was rude, ugly and smelled."

"Wow, that's a lot of bad stuff first thing in the morning Beryl."

"If you see him, avoid him, Jamie, he is evil."

"How will I know him?"

"He drives a Black shiny van, and he has a big nose."

"What." cried Jamie, as he stared at the girl, not believing what he had heard. She looked at him saying. "Jamie, what's wrong you look like you've seen a ghost."

"See you Beryl" he squeezed out, then fled with his arms full of Bakery food. Beryl watched him run to the Bentley, jump in and the car drove quickly away. She just stood open mouthed, staring at it disappearing down the road to the Golf club.

Back in the Bentley. Al said. "What took you so long Jamie?" "He's here." shouted Jamie.

"Who's bloody here?" Barked the Colonel.

"Black Van man." croaked Jamie.

"What" the Colonel shouted, stopping the Bentley hard, causing other cars to honk their horns at him.

"What did you say boy?"

"Sir he upset Beryl this morning in the Bakery, he smells and he's got a big nose."

Al chipped in with. "No doubt he uses his big nose to smell with Jamie."

"This is serious Al." The Colonel said rebuking him.

"Tell us the full story Jamie, don't leave anything out."

Jamie, having now recovered a little, related the whole conversation that he'd had previously with Beryl.

Then added. "I think it's Pastor Williams Sir, I just remembered that Wendy told me that he took the van when he left their Mum, and he had a big Nose, didn't he Al."

"Yes Jamie he did, he stuck it right in my face that day on the Mountain, and he smelt awful."

The Colonel restarted the Bentley and drove to the Golf Club with his usual aggression, all the while giving instructions to the three passengers.

Arriving at the clubhouse, they all went about their prearranged duties, while the Colonel got on the phone to Ted Dexter. "Ted, that Black Van has turned up here today, it's that Idiot Welsh Pastor, we need you to join us in hunting him down, we'll talk when you get here pal."

Ted replied. "I'm leaving now Sir."

Jamie had run to the Club Shop to use the other phone, where he had rung to speak to Stewart Williams in Wales, he asked him if he knew the registration number of the Parish van that Mr Williams had taken when he left. He was now waiting for a return call from Wales.

Al and Dave were busy arranging things for the Tournament that day, and both the girls, Beryl and Rachel were soon to arrive and organise the food for the Dinner dance.

Some time later, Ted Dexter arrived and was with Jamie when the return call came from Wales, they now had all of the required Registration details of the van.

"It is officially Grey, so he has painted it Black to try to avoid detection." Ted told the Colonel.

"Thanks for coming down Ted, but it's all about your two boys, so you should be involved, let's get this Club day over with and we can concentrate on the crazy Welshman tomorrow.

The golf Tournament went off without any trouble and Al took out the prize for Juniors, but he had to put up with Beryl telling him that he was lucky that she only had one arm, because she had won it twice in the past.

The Dinner dance that followed, was successful with Jamie and Rachel putting on a dance masterclass for the members.

After cleaning up and making sure that all was well with the Clubhouse and Shop, The Colonel told the crew to all go home and rest.

As he was getting in the Bentley, Dave whispered in his ear. "Sir, as I was saying goodbye to Sally I spotted a dark coloured van leaving the car park just now."

"Thanks Dave, don't tell the young ones, but I'll let Dexter know when we get home, it looks like he's stalking the boys."

Later that night Ted, Dave and The Colonel were having a night cap in the office, catching up with the latest news about the stalking. Ted volunteered to do first shift in guarding the Mansion, Dave would relieve him at three in the morning, Robertson thanked them both, then said. "Tomorrow we will hunt down this crazy Welsh Pastor and put him away."

**Day one,** and everyone at the Mansion was up early and were all at the breakfast table when The Colonel spoke. "We think that Williams is stalking both of the boys, we know why, but that is immaterial as he has broken the law, we will work in three teams as we search for him."

"Ted and Al, are team number one, they can search the outskirts of the Town in Ted's Jeep, Dave and Olly will do foot patrol, in and around the shopping centre, and Jamie and I will do the inner residential area in the Bentley."

Ted got up and said. "Al and I are ready to go now Sir."

As they were about to leave, Betty ran into the room and told the Colonel. "Mr Rogers hasn't turned up yet Sir, what about the Mink?"

Robertson replied. "Let's all go and check out the animals first, then we can proceed to search for Taffy, Dave will you ring Rogers and find out what's wrong?"

Al was first to the Farm door, he went to unlock it, but it was already half open. He looked up at Robertson questioningly. "What the?" he cried, pushing the door further open and running in to be met by a total mess.

Whoever had been in the Farm that night had caused havoc, some of the cages were open, Mink were missing, some lay dead on the floor, others could be seen clambering over the shelves of food containers.

The Colonel was devastated. He told Olly to go and ring the Police, then asked all of the crew to help him catch the escaped Mink and put them back in their cages.

Eventually order was restored, the local Police arrived at the same time as Rogers.

Robertson asked Rogers. "Why are you so late?"

He answered. "Some devil slashed my tyres during the night, I had to ring the garage for four new ones, then I rang Morrison to tell him about it, and he offered me a lift here in the Police car, I'm sorry Colonel, I've no idea what has happened in the Farm, it was in perfect order yesterday afternoon when I left.

Robertson told Rogers about the Welshman, who was of course, now a suspect in the death of the Mink and Roger's tyre slashing episode.

Sgt. Morrison took the details of the Pastors Van, saying that he would put a stolen vehicle notice for all County Police to apprehend the driver.

They left Rogers to clean up the mess in the Farm, and assist the police when necessary.

The three teams separated and commenced to patrol their given Areas, they were looking for any coloured Van and any one with a large nose that spoke with a Welsh accent.

Jamie sat next to the Colonel in the Bentley, thinking that the car wasn't really a good search vehicle, as it attracted far too much attention to itself, but it was no use telling The Colonel that.

They spotted a couple of Vans and they followed a Black one all the way to the Bakery, The local Electrician jumped out and asked the Colonel why he was being followed.

"Sorry Saunders old chap, but we are a bit on edge today." "That's OK, Colonel, we all get like that sometimes." They saw Baker outside his shop and waved.

"Haven't seen that other Black van have you?"

"No Sir, Beryl told me about the stalker. the devil was in my shop yesterday" "If you guys spot him again Baker, ring Sgt. Morrison straight away."

"I certainly will Sir, I've got something to say to him myself."


Olly and Dave were patrolling the Shops, and car parks in the centre of Etchingham, Dave was busy chatting to all the young ladies, and Olly was stuffing himself with goodies from the many food shops.

"No blooming Vans around here Dave, except the delivery ones and I know every driver in Etchingham."

"I don't think the Mad Welshman will come near this part of town, he's probably driven up to Burwash or Hurst Green."

"The Cops have his number now Dave, they'll get him way before we see him."

"He must be really crazy, to do that to the Mink and slash Rogers tyres."

"I hope he's not armed, If he sees Al or Jamie he could attack them."

"Captain Dexter won't have any trouble disarming him, but the Colonel ain't as young and spritely as he used to be,"

"I've been giving the boys unarmed combat lessons at the Lodge at night, Al's a natural and Jamie is smart and is picking it up OK."


Ted Dexter and Al, were cruising the streets where the Van was most unlikely to be, Al questioned his Dad. "Do you think that he would be hanging around the Town after what he did last night, Dad."

"No Al, not really, but we have to make sure, then we can broaden our search to include the local villages and other possible hiding places, like the woods and the like."

"I'm starting to get hungry, it's been hours since Breakfast."

"The Colonel suggested we all go back to the Manor for lunch at one."

"Good, because my watch says twelve thirty."

"OK buddy we might as well drive towards home now."

Back at the Mansion, the three crews met for lunch, and discussed the problems involved in searching for the Van.

They decided to continue patrolling the areas as before until dark, they would then all return to the Mansion for Dinner and a good rest.

It was Midnight, and Williams had just parked his Black Van in a wooded area at the back of the Etchingham Station, he was concealing it with branches, and other vegetation.

When he had finished he started to walk back towards the Town along High St. He saw a Morris Eight parked near the Post Office, and had no trouble breaking in and starting the motor, he then drove straight to Hurst Green and hid the Morris behind a disused warehouse.

Then he walked around the area looking for another vehicle, seeing a Motorbike, he checked it for petrol, climbed on and rode off to Dale Hill Hotel and Golf Course, which was in the other direction.

Then he dumped the Bike in bushes behind the Hotel, and chose a shiny Red Riley Sports car, he broke in and drove it back to Etchingham Station.

Parking the Riley next to the Van, he climbed into the Van with the intention of going to sleep.

He lay, thinking about the Wild Goose chase that the Police would have on their hands in the morning looking for all of the stolen vehicles, and would therefore not be able to concentrate on searching for him, but of course he hadn't taken in to account the fact that four experienced civilians and two very smart boys were also looking for him.

**Day Two.** Ted Dexter asked The Colonel. "Do you think we should expand the search outside the town, as he seems to have disappeared into thin air Sir."

"Yes of course Ted, You take your two boys, and Dave and Olly can ride with me."

"Good idea Sir. I'll search the East side of the County, and perhaps you could look at the west side."

"Yes Ted, and we can all meet back here at the end of the day." All agreed, and they headed off to continue the search.

During the day, Robertson called into the Police Station to ask if any progress had been made in the search for the stolen Van.

Sergeant Morrison told him angrily. "Colonel the county is suffering from a spate of stolen vehicles, from all over the place. It doesn't make sense, some are missing, others are left unharmed, just in the wrong place."

"So I take it that's a no to my question."

"Sorry mate but I have no men to spare, the Superintendent's Riley is missing, that unfortunately it is a priority. It was stolen from the Dale Hill Hotel in the middle of the night, he actually lives in Battle, it's all very embarrassing for him."

The Colonel, Dave and Olly all left with smiles on their faces, Dave said. "We are not going to get any help from the constabulary until that car comes back."

"Yes it looks like we are on our own chaps."

That evening at dinner everyone was joking about the Riley, Olly told them all that the car actually belonged to the Superintendents Wife.

This little bit of news brought more laughter from everyone.

After the meal, both Al and Jamie had gone up to bed. Robertson said. "Well guys it seems that we have to continue without any help, so we'll just do the same thing tomorrow as today."

Dave suggested that perhaps Williams had decided that he had done enough damage to everyone, and gone home.

"You could well be right Dave, but I think this Madman has not done with this bout of destruction, as he hasn't ventured near the boys yet."

"You're correct Colonel, I am very conscious of the fact that he really wants to hurt the lads,"

Robertson asked them all. "Please let's make a concerted effort tomorrow, I feel that time is running out,"

With that they all went to bed, except Olly, who was on first watch.

**Day Three.** Dulcie Widmark, accompanied by daughter Rachel and her friend Beryl got on the Train at Etchingham Station at Eight Thirty in the morning, Dulcie was taking the girls to the Opera House in Tunbridge Wells, to watch a Musical being staged by their High School.

Colonel Robertson and Captain Dexter spent the whole day with their crews, searching through the County for a sign of the Black Van, totally disappointed, they returned to the Mansion around six P.M.

After dinner, Robertson addressed the crew. "Well it looks like he's flown the coop for now, we'd best all think about returning to our jobs tomorrow."

He added. "Dave and I will remain here at the Mansion, keeping a close watch over Al and Jamie.

Once again, the adults agreed that it was the sensible thing to do.

The boys went up to their room, disappointed that the search was going to be called off.

Jamie told Al. "I'm still going to look for him, I don't think that he has gone away, he's already been unstoppable, why should he give up now?"

The train from Tunbridge Wells was running late that evening, due to a problem further up the line, this caused Dulcie and the girls to be late getting in to Etchingham Station.

Beryl had been looking out of the carriage window as the train slowly pulled into the platform, when her attention was drawn to what looked like a vehicle partly covered in branches, away from the main car park, it was almost hidden by bushes and trees, she felt a shiver go down her spine as she was sure that it was Black, and a Van.

She hurriedly joined the other two on leaving the carriage. She ran up to Dulcie and started to tell her about the vehicle. Rachel said. "Beryl, you have become obsessed with this Van lately, how could you say that it was the Pastors Van, it's dark now."

"Well, maybe I am a bit uptight about it, but there was a dark vehicle in those bushes."

Dulcie told the girls. "It's too late to do anything now, maybe I'll ring The Colonel when we get home." Then they got into her car and she drove to the Bakery to drop Beryl off, then drove to her own house.

She decided that it was too late now to ring the Mansion, she new that the men had been out all day searching.

**Day Four.** Breakfast at the Mansion and Ted Dexter spoke to Olly. "I can give you a lift to the Golf Club on my way back to London, Olly."

"Thank you Sir, I guess the member's will be glad to get their barman back again."

Robertson guffawed at that remark saying. "Do them good to go dry now and then, might improve their Golf scores."

Al told the Colonel. "The phones ringing in your office Sir." "Will you get it Al, your quicker than me?"

Al was already halfway to the Office, and continued to hurry.

He called out. "It's for you Colonel, It's Mrs Widmark sir, she says it's urgent." He virtually ran to his office mumbling something or other under his breath. He smartly returned to the table, after talking to Dulcie.

"Young Beryl swears that she saw the Van parked in bushes at the back of the Etchingham Station last night."

All six of the search party stood up from the table and headed for their vehicles.

The plan was to go straight to the Car park at the station and they would decide tactics there.

On arriving near the Station, Robertson asked Dexter to take Dave and Olly to establish whether it was the Black Van, they approached stealthily, Dave looked in the window of the Van, he decided that it was unoccupied, Dexter told him to break in and start the vehicle, which he did, they removed all of the camouflage that was covering it, then Dave drove it in convoy with the other two cars to the Police Station.

Sgt Morrison looked in amazement at the Van, thanked the Colonel and the rest of the crew, for their vigilance, then told them that all the missing vehicles had now been found, except the Superintendent's Riley.

Robertson said. "Then that's what he is driving, and he must still be in Etchingham. We'll go back to the Mansion and regroup, we must catch this guy now."

They drove to the Mansion in time for lunch. The Colonel went looking for Betty to rustle up something quick so that they could get back out to search

"Where the bloody hell is she when you need her?" he barked.

Al and Jamie were searching high and low for her, Jamie had a thought that she might be in the Mink farm helping Rogers, so he investigated.

He ran back into the house shouting. "Colonel, Mr Rogers is knocked out and tied up,"

Robertson exploded with. "Someone ring that fool Morrison, and tell him my home has been violated again."

Al told him. "Sir, Betty is missing, her handbag and purse are on the kitchen table and her coat is hanging up."

"Probably been abducted by that Lunatic Williams."

Dave and Olly had unbound Rogers and had him laying on a couch in the great room.

Dave told Robertson. "He was hit from behind with a blunt instrument, he has a huge lump on his head. I recommend that he go to Hospital Sir, he could have bleeding on the brain."

"OK Dave, you organise that, we need to find Betty before that madman hurts her."

Jamie ran into the room shouting. "Williams is on the phone in your office sir."

"Bloody cheek of the man, I'll straighten him out right now." as he stormed off to the phone.

He returned very meekly. "He wants a swap. Betty for the Boys."

Dexter bellowed. "Not likely, I'll strangle the idiot if I get my hands on him."

"I know how you feel Ted, I'm the same, where the devil is Sgt Morrison?"

Jamie called out. "Sergeant Morrison's on the phone now sir."

"Good, let's go into my office and hear what he has to say."

Picking up the phone, he opened up with. "What about some help up here Morrison?"

"Colonel, A Detective Sergeant is on his way to you right now, he will have a team with him to manage with the Telephone etcetera, by the way the Riley has been returned, it was left outside the Pie Shop, near the Police Station."

"The cheek of the man. He truly must be insane. Now we have no idea what vehicle he is using." The Colonel Grunted.

The Sergeant replied with, "I will let you know as soon as we get a stolen vehicle report, and I'll go to the Hospital and question Rogers about the attack, I'll update you when I can Sir."


Two Police cars stopped outside the Mansion, Detective Sergeant Watkins in one car and Sergeant Smyth and Constable Carter in the second vehicle. They were met at the door by Olly and ushered in to the now crowded Office.

Robertson was happy to see three officers allocated to the job. He bellowed. "Welcome gentlemen, we are badly in need of some experienced help."

"My pleasure Colonel, Sergeant Smyth and Carter will set up the telephone intercept, for when the suspect rings back."

Everyone waited for the phone to ring, it seemed like an eternity, when it did, everybody leapt to their feet excitedly.

Robertson picked up the phone and answered.

"Fat Betty Lawton is becoming very stressed out Colonel, and she wants to be swapped for those nasty little tykes." Crooned Williams.

"Now look Williams, just release my housekeeper, she is an innocent party and it is a most unchristian act that you have committed considering that you profess to be a man of God."

"Rubbish Robertson, I have a direct line to him, I am his disciple, now let's discuss the swap."

Detective Watkins whispered in The Colonel's ear. "Try to keep him talking Sir, we may be able to get a trace on the call."

Robertson nodded and continued with. "I Implore you Pastor Williams, for the benefit of you own two children, the sweet and lovely Wendy and your smart son Stewart, release Betty, I'm sure that she won't press kidnapping charges if you let her go now."

"How generous of you, washed up soldier that you are, keep your nose out of my family affairs, that brat Al kidnapped my dear Wendy and brainwashed her into believing that he was good for her, you are all the evil ones and justice will rain on you in the end." Then the line went dead.

"He's gone Sergeant, I must of upset him a little, sorry."

"It's not your fault Colonel, it's quiet obvious that the man is totally insane, anything will provoke him, we need to find a means to track him down, let's spend the time between now and when he next rings to use our imaginations in finding a way,

There were no further phone calls from Williams that night, the crew retired early, including the Policemen, they hardly needed anyone on watch tonight, with two police cars parked outside.

Day Five. Jamie was up early, he rode his bike to the Bakery, with no Betty to cook Breakfast for the Crew, he had decided that Pies, Sausage Rolls and fresh bread would go down well.

He barged into the Bakery, seeing Rachel and Beryl alone in the shop, he jokingly called out. "Can I have some service please young ladies."

"Jamie, it's so nice to see you, have you guys caught that madman yet?"

"No Rachel, he's kidnapped Betty and put Rogers in hospital, he's a really crazy man, you girls shouldn't be in here alone."

With that, Beryl produced a cricket bat from under the counter, she waived it around energetically, saying. "I can't wait for him to walk in that door Jamie, I'm itching to break a bone or two."

"You're a tough one Beryl, I don't know how Al handles you."
"Al doesn't handle me, we are just very good friends."

Jamie smirked at her and replied. "I've been thinking about Williams, if he is in vehicles all the time he must be having snacks and Pies to eat."

"Well he won't come in here again, so he must be getting his food from the other Pie Shop, near the Police Station or Millie's Cafe near the Train Station."

"Are they the only places in town that do that sort of food?" Queried Jamie.

Beryl thought, then answered. "Yes, but I don't think he would go near the Police Station again, after leaving the Superintendent's Wife's Riley there yesterday."

Jamie said excitedly. "That's right, and he probably got food at the Shop when he was there, Girls I have to go, please give me my order for the men's breakfast, and I'll be off."

He hurried back to the Mansion, put the food in the kitchen, and went looking for Al, he found him in the Mink Farm and whispered in his ear. "I think I know where he might be hiding."

"Jamie, are you going on another wild goose chase?"

"No Al, I'm serious, he must be eating takeaway food all the time, he can't go to the Bakery now, and the Pie Shop is too close to the Police Station."

"So? Where is he getting food?"

"Millie's Cafe near the Train Station, and there's a telephone box right next door, that must be where he is ringing from."

"We have to tell the men, they'll know what to do."

"No, we can do an undercover search, then come back and tell them."

"So what do you think we should do about it Jamie?"

"Let's put our Hoody Parkas on and ride our bikes past the area, looking for cars parked anywhere near, then ride back here and tell the Colonel."

"Sounds OK, if Williams does happen to see us he wont know who we are," "Let's go now Al, before everybody is about, I grabbed our five irons out of the bags, just in case."

They wheeled their bikes onto the road and pedalled hurriedly down towards the Station.

Olly was feeding the Mink in the Farm and watching Dave who was looking out of the window, he called out. "aren't you going to do any work today Dave?"

"Sorry Olly, I was watching the two boys riding off somewhere, and I was trying to decide whether I should tell the boss."

"You certainly should Dave, he will go nuts if he doesn't know where they are, and their Dad will likely go right off at you."

Dave ran into the house shouting. "The boys road off on their bikes Sir, should we follow them?"

"What the hell do they think they're doing? I'll Get the Jeep and follow them, which way did they go Dave?"

"Down the main road sir, maybe towards the Train Station?"

Ted Dexter leapt into the jeep, waited for Dave and Sgt Smyth to join him, then set of after the boys.

Jamie and Al rode past Millie's Cafe, slowing down to peep inside. Jamie called out. "He's not in there Al, let's go down the road a bit and turn around."

Al caught up with him, shouting, "Someone walked into the phone box, after we road past, he had a hood on, it could be him."

Jamie raced back towards the Phone Box, bellowing. "It's him Al, Betty must be here somewhere."

Williams had heard the familiar voice of an excited Jamie, he ran out of the Box towards a car that was parked behind Millie's Cafe.

Jamie was in full pursuit on his bike, waiving his five iron in an effort to scare Williams, while shouting at him. "Let Betty go Williams you coward, then face up to me and Al."

Hearing that shouted at him, his temper flared and he turned and ran straight at the boy on the bike, colliding with him and sending both of them to the ground.

Al arrived, jumped off his bike and stood over the now prostrate Williams, threatening him with his Number five iron, The Pastor was in no condition to protest, he had landed hard on his back and was in a world of pain.

Jamie struggled to get up and dusted himself off then joined his brother in threatening Williams.

The Jeep ground to a halt feet away from the boys, Ted Dexter leapt out and grabbed Williams by the throat, whispering to him. "If that policeman wasn't here I would throttle you until you screamed for mercy."

Sergeant Smyth allowed Ted to get rid of his anger first, then he handcuffed the snivelling Ex Pastor.

Dave called out from behind the Cafe. "Betty is here in the Car, she's fine, so she said."

The Sergeant called the Police Station, requesting a local Officer take the prisoner to Jail, He waited for them with Williams, now handcuffed, and still whining.

Ted and Dave returned to the Mansion, Dave holding poor Betty who was overjoyed at having been found. The two heroes rode behind on their bikes.

Ted Dexter, The Colonel and the Detective Sergeant, all roasted both boys for daring to ride off and expose themselves to danger.

"What the devil were you thinking, Al, you should have known better?" Jamie admitted that he had talked Al into it, so he should take the blame, he added. "We had no intention of approaching Williams, but he heard me calling to Al and he ran at me."

Then Betty produced two large plates full of Cakes and goodies for her heroes to enjoy.

Al rang Wendy and Stewart in Wales, to tell them what had eventuated, and said that he was sorry about their dad being Jailed, but he had done some really bad things, he also told them that they could come and pickup their Parish Van.

A week later, Both Stewart and Wendy arrived and stayed for a few days at the Mansion with the boys, then they took possession of the Van and drove it back to their Village in Wales.

✧ ✧ ✧

# CHAPTER 13

It wasn't long before both boys became bored again with village life, School, then Golf and the occasional weekend at Hastings, both Beryl and Rachel accompanied them almost everywhere they went, which was a bit of icing on the cake for them.

One particular day they where walking home from School on the way to the Bakery, to tuck into the few remaining cakes left over from the days sales, which they did most schooldays.

Jamie was his usual quiet self when Rachel asked him. "Why are you so unsociable today, Jamie?"

"I'm not really, it's just that I am wondering why all of the Army trucks that are constantly driving through town are Americans?"

Al jumped in with. "They happen to be our Allies Jamie, isn't it obvious?"

"Al, you are so basic in your thinking, it's almost impossible to believe that we are brothers." retaliated Jamie.

Al took a friendly swipe at him, then said. "So Mr genius what's your thoughts on it?"

"Well brother, The War is now being fought in Italy, Greece and Russia, you might even have noticed that the Nazi bombings are much less, it's because Hitler is very busy elsewhere."

"Maybe they will be going to fight against Rommel then."

"I heard that he had been sent back to Germany, after they lost at El-Alemein." "They would be sailing from Portsmouth or over that side, if they were going to the Adriatic."

"Well I can't help you Jamie, you will have to talk to Winston Churchill he would know."

The girls started to giggle, all of the boys conversations went the same way in the end.

Jamie just smiled condescendingly at Al, as they had reached the Bakery and the smell of freshly baked bread and pies took preference.

At dinner that evening Jamie asked The Colonel. "Do you think that Jerry will try to invade us, Sir?"

"What made you ask that question young man?"

"Well Sir, the town is full of American troops, and I don't think that they are going anywhere from this part of the country."

Robertson looked at Jamie studiously, he answered carefully. "Jamie, it is so enlightening that you are such a studious person, but you must not try to read something into every troop movement that takes place, and you most certainly must not talk about it, you never know who may be listening."

"But Sir, we are alone here, unless Betty has turned to spying for Hitler."

"I doubt that Jamie, Hitler is the reason that her hubby is overseas fighting."

"Isn't it alright to talk here?"

"Well Yes, but be careful in future, and no, I don't think that there will be any invasion because he missed his chance when he opened the Eastern front."

"Then are we thinking about invading France?"

"Robertson was stunned by the perception of this child, he took hold of Jamie's hand and asked him gently. "Please Jamie, try to give all of your attention to either, School, Golf or young

Rachel, but stop worrying about worldwide issues, we have Mr Churchill and President Roosevelt to worry about these things."

Jamie then took his turn in looking straight into the Colonels eyes, saying. "Then I take it is a Yes, Sir?"

"Damn Hell, what a child, Which Planet are you from Jamie?"

"You can tell me and Al Sir, we will keep it a secret and never talk about it outside, Scouts Honour."

"Botheration Jamie, you are the limit, I might as well tell you what I know, then you must swear that you will say not one word to anyone, not even your sweethearts."

The Colonel then sat the boys down in his Office and told them that there was to be an offensive, probably in the South of France. Then he asked them both to swear silence, which they did happily.


Next morning, Al asked if they could go down to Hastings for the weekend, as Beryl was having her Birthday Party there.

"Of course lads I'll drop you there after school today, you must try to relax now and enjoy life."

"Thank you Sir." Both boys chirped, then started to discuss what clothing they would take. Al told Jamie. "Don't forget your deodorant, Jamie." Then he winked at him, grinning like the cat that got the milk.

The poor boy, shrugged, then retorted. "Why Al, have you used up all of yours again."

Al realised that Jamie was going to win out in the end, so he pretended to be distracted while searching for something.

They were both excited to be able to spend the weekend with the Girls, and were looking forward to swimming in the Channel once again.

School passed quickly and before long they were sitting in the Bentley on their way.

Mrs. Baker had decorated the Holiday House for Beryls Birthday, and everyone was in party mood.

Saturday morning and all four were running towards the beach, ready for a swim, when they arrived, they discovered that it had been sealed off with barbed wire.

Al shouted. "What's going on, where can we swim?"

He was answered by a soldier, carrying a rifle on the other side of the fence. "Not here laddy, the whole beach is closed all along the south coast."

The four all stood and looked through the wire fence at what was going on, hundreds of soldiers were running up the beach in full gear, then walking back down to the edge of the water, then, on command they ran up again.

Jamie moaned. "Well that's the end of our beach day, let's go into town and buy some goodies for the party."

They trudged off, complaining about American soldiers taking over their beach.

Jamie and Al, looked at each other knowingly and did their best to distract the girls, with Al saying. "It looks like we will have to start the party early, but I'm all for that, so after we get some sweets, we can go back to the house and start the games."

On the way home they stopped at the top of the cliff where Jamie used to watch the boats, and were surprised at the number of soldiers on the beaches all along, as far as they could see.

Jamie kept looking up and down the cliffs, towards the Fishing Port, where he concentrated on a couple looking down at the beaches with binoculars, a man and a woman. He told the others that he would watch for a while, as they went off chomping on sweets.

He took out his little notebook, which he always carried, and started writing, when he had finished he ran off and caught up with the others as they were going into the house.

The party for Beryl was only small but she had her best friends with her so she was happy, they played all sorts of games, as they were all very competitive by nature, so it went on for all hours, eventually Reg Baker suggested that they all go to bed. As he was going to drive them back to Etchingham early in the morning, because the beach and surrounds were out of bounds to all civilians now.

Jamie went straight to the Colonel's office when he got home and gave him his notebook to read.

Robertson now took Jamie very seriously about everything military, saying. "Good work Jamie, I'm glad that you are still watching out for our country, leave this with me and I'll ring my contacts straight away, then we'll all go up to the Club and have a days Golf, do you want me to pick up your young ladies on the way?"

Al replied immediately. "Yes please Sir, we need some competition."

Jamie chirped. "You mean, you do, I think Beryl is giving you lessons secretly."

The Colonel told them. "Wait for me in the car, I wont be on the phone too long."

They picked up the Girls and spent all of the afternoon Golfing and talking, eventually they ended up in the club rooms, drinking lemonade and eating cakes.

The Colonel signalled for Jamie to come to the Office where he whispered to him. "Good work yesterday my boy, both of the parties that were using binoculars were arrested, and had notes on them that said that the American General Patton, was located with his Army in Kent. This was classified as Secret. My contact said that I should recommend you for an award."

"Sir, I'm so glad that they were spies, I thought that everyone would laugh at me in the Home Office."

"What about the Award, Jamie?"

"No Sir, Everyone at school thinks that I have a big head already, since the last arrest."

"You will be getting recognised for your work, we will keep it under wraps until a suitable time, OK?"

"Yes Sir, but please don't tell Al, he will never stop harassing me."

"Jamie, your brother is secretly so proud of you, he will be the first to congratulate you."

"When will it happen Sir?"

"Your Award or the Invasion?" "No Sir, the invasion."

Colonel Robertson looked at Jamie and said. "Tomorrow, the Sixth of June, You and Al will be with me and my colleagues on the beach head watching the whole event from midnight tonight, so go and get your brother, wrap yourselves up and join me in the Bentley."

The drive to the coast was exciting for the boys, they were going to be with some of the top brass watching all night.

They arrived, to be welcomed by the senior officers who were detailed to observe happenings and report back in the morning.

Around Midnight the bombers flew over the channel and bombed near Cherbourg, the sky was lit up by the Bombing and the German artillery fire.

More planes flew past the coast and kept going, the Colonel told the boys that they had Parachutists on board to land in France and take key towns.

Later in the morning, British and American Battleships and Cruisers, bombarded the target beaches.

Then around daybreak the Landing Barges appeared out of the gloom and headed for the beaches.

The Carnage went on all day, finally, Colonel Robertson decided to take the boys home. The effect of that night would live in their memories forever,

✦ ✦ ✦

# CHAPTER 14

The Seventh of June Nineteen Forty Four, everyone awakened to the news that the Invasion of France had begun and there was a sense of joy everywhere in town.

Al and Jamie missed school that day and slept in.

They were awakened by Betty telling them that two young ladies were at the front door to escort them to Golf.

Rachel asked Jamie. "Why are you two so sleepy today, we missed you at school?"

"You won't believe this, but Colonel Robertson took us down the coast to watch the invasion from our side, we were there all night."

Beryl cried. "It must have been an incredible sight."

"It was absolutely frightening really, I can't get it out of my head." Replied Jamie.

They told the girls all about the Invasion that they were able to see, which put the Golf on the back burner for the day, so they just sat around the Clubhouse talking.

Al told the girls that now the Invasion was on, their Mum would probably want Him and Jamie home again, which made them all sad.

When the boys returned to the Mansion that evening, They were asked to go into the Office with The Colonel.

Al whispered to Jamie. "I bet its about us going home."

Unfortunately Al didn't whisper quietly enough, as the Colonel broke into laughter, saying. "Al, you were nearly right, In fact Ted Dexter rang me today to tell me he has been given a posting to the British Embassy in Washington. He is expected to take Mrs Dexter with him. So he has asked me to put up with you two rascals until they return, which could easily be at the end of the War."

Al asked. "Did he get promoted Sir?"

"Yes boys, your Dad is now a Major, which is a senior rank." Jamie asked. "Will we be able to see them before they go?"

"Of course Jamie, I will drive you up to London next week and we can stay for a few days then see them off."

"Thank you sir, Who will look after our house then?"

"They will probably allow the Army to rent it out to another Officer and his family, maybe the one who is coming back from our Embassy in the US.

"Then we will have to take all of our stuff from when we where kids, like clothes and toys."

"No Jamie, that can all go into Storage, or you can bring your toys if you need them." Robertson crooned, while smiling at Al.

"Colonel Sir, I'm not a baby, but I still want to hang on to some of my favourite things."

"I know that neither of you Dexter boys are babies, you are both very brave and intelligent young men." Robertson proudly declared.

Then he told them that they could to use the phone and ring the Girls to tell them that they were going to be around for a long time yet.

There were a lot more smiling faces around Town, the Allies were advancing on Germany, the Russians a little quicker than on the Eastern border, so Hitler sent many of his troops from France to The East, this helped to speed up the invasion in France.

The Girls were glad to have the Dexter boys back in their classrooms and as opponents on the Golf course.

The only concern now was that Rachel continually worried about her Dad, he had been transferred from Naval Operations to Fleet action, and he was now commanding a Cruiser attached to the Australian Fleet in the Pacific Ocean, fighting the Japanese. There didn't seem to be an end to the war there.

Al had Talked the Colonel into allowing the Girls to come with them to London to see Ted Dexter off.

Di welcomed them all and took them up to their rooms, then they all sat down to a Roast Dinner.

Later the Foursome sat in the Boys rooms and helped them sort out the stuff that they wanted to take back to Etchingham, there was a lot of giggling from both girls as they sorted through Jamie's old toys.

When they had finished there, they all went down to help pack up Di's belongings, as she was coming back to the Mansion to stay, until it was time for her to go to the States.

The following morning they all watched as Ted climbed aboard an American Airforce plane at a country Airfield, it took off with an escort of two fighters to see it safely out over the Atlantic Ocean.

Because of the slow progress of the Allied Forces in France, A decision was made to slow down the production of Arms and Ammunition in Germany, The City of Hamburg was saturated with bombs by the Allied Air Forces, killing some Twenty Thousand Civilians in one night.

This was followed by an even larger Air Bombardment on the City of Dresden, virtually annihilating the whole area, by turning it into a fireball, killing as many as Twenty five thousand.

The German civilian spirit was broken,

Even so the Russian Army was first to Berlin, they Raped the City, to the disgust of the rest of the world.

Order returned when the Allied Troops arrived and the Berlin was divided into East and West.

The German Generals had gladly Surrendered, there was now Peace in Europe. The whole of the United Kingdom celebrated.

Jamie tried desperately to cheer up Rachel, she was missing her Dad as he was still commanding his warship in the Pacific.

Finally she relaxed when her Mum told her. "Dad's on his way back from Australia, he should be home next week."

Rachel was sad for the Japanese civilians, as the Bombing of Hiroshima was dreadful, then it was followed by the second Bombing of Nagasaki, bringing the Japs to the negotiating table.

Finally Peace in the Pacific, World Peace.

Ted Dexter had returned from the US. and resigned his commission, he had subsequently been recruited by the Diplomatic Corp, and was to return to Washington, as Assistant to the Ambassador.

Al was the first to leave the Mansion, as he had applied for a place in the Military Academy, this was supported by both His Father and Colonel Robertson.

He told his friends. "I would have probably got in on my own good record, but it was handy to have a Dad who was a senior Officer in the Army, and of course The Colonel with all his mates in the Defence Department.

His Family and Beryl, saw him of at Tunbridge Wells Station, he wasn't going too far away, he told Beryl that he would come down every leave and see her, The Colonel had also told him that he would always be welcome at the Mansion.

Commander Widmark, having returned to England also resigned his Commission and was offered a position with the

Australian Naval Department, so he planned to return there as quickly as possible, then he would send for Dulcie and Rachel after finding a house.

Everything was happening, friends were leaving for different parts of the World.

Jamie was in a quandary, he did not want to go to America with his Mum and Dad.

Di spent some time trying to convince him that he would like life in the States. He replied. "Mum, I will never go to America, I'm sorry but I wish Dad had gone for a Post in a nicer country."

Di angrily replied. "America was our biggest Allie, Jamie."

"Only towards the end of the war mum, they are always last in, we were nearly invaded because they wouldn't help."

"You must talk to your father about this my Lad, I give up."

"I want to go to Australia, Mum. I can immigrate, if I find a person there to nominate me, I know because my friend at school, Michael has gone to live with his sister there."

"Jamie, you don't know anyone in Australia."

"What about Rachel's Dad?"

"Oh, so that's the story, you want to follow your girlfriend there?"

"No it's not that, yes I do like Rachel a lot but It's the country that I am interested in, it's the best place to live right now, there are lot's of opportunities for young people to find work."

"Do you actually think Mr Widmark will support you financially until you get a job?"

"I was hoping that Dad and you would."

Di was exasperated, she was floundering, it was almost impossible to argue with this boy, she spoke to him quietly. "Jamie, we will discuss this tonight at home with your Father."

"OK Mum, thanks for listening, I love you, your the best Mum in the whole wide World."

That evening Ted Dexter listened to his youngest son, give him a reason not to accompany them to America.

"Jamie, I can't believe that you can hate a country so much as you do America."

"Dad, please let me go and live in Australia."

"You're Mother says that you want to go and stay with the Widmarks."

"Yes Dad. Mister Widmark said that I can go with them when Dulcie and Rachel go."

"I need to talk to Eric and Dulcie first, I'll let you know our decision later, now just go and enjoy yourself with your buddies."

Jamie ran off to find Rachel and Beryl, they talked about Australia for hours. Later, His Dad called Jamie in and told him that they had agreed that he could go to Australia with the Widmarks.

He was overjoyed, he ran out to find Rachel and tell her the good news. "I know Jamie, Dad just told me that they have agreed, He and Mum will nominate you and we will be living in the same house over there."

"What do you know about Sydney Rachel?"

"It's the biggest city in Australia and it has a huge bridge and a massive harbour where the Navel Fleet is."

It was now time for The Dexter's to leave for Washington, they had sent for their daughter Beth to be sent to Etchingham from Auntie Jeans in Scotland, because she, was certainly going with them to Washington. A large number of friends and relatives saw them Board The Queen Mary, the usual streamers and tears accompanied them.

Then the massive Vessel was moved away from the Pier with the aid of three tugs, And it sailed off into the sunset, across the Atlantic Ocean to New York.

Dulcie and Eric Widmark had sold the family home in Etchingham, and they would use the proceeds to buy a property in Sydney.

Eric left for Sydney on the Fairsky, a P&O passenger ship carrying immigrants to all parts of Australia, it was only two weeks after Jamie's parents had left for Washington.

Di, Rachel and Jamie, waited patiently for their turn to come, they had been put on a waiting list, with the thousands of other people waiting to Immigrate to Australia.

Finally the parcel arrived with their Boarding passes, luggage tags and baggage stickers, also instructions on how to get to Tilbury Docks in London, and which needles they needed to have to board ship.

They busied themselves with going to the Doctor for their Injections, and Medicals, then they said their goodbye's to their many friends.

Colonel Robertson drove them and Beryl to Tilbury, A few tears where shed by the Girls, then the three of them walked up the steps along the side of the ship and disappeared inside.

Some time later they reappeared on deck and waived to Beryl and The Colonel, Rachel and Jamie threw streamers down to them, which they hung on to until the Ocean Liner, RMS Mooltan slipped away into the Estuary of the Thames and down towards the English Channel.

✧ ✧ ✧

# CHAPTER 15

Jamie awoke, to find the Mooltan, rolling from side to side, then front to back. He leapt out of his bunk bed, only to be confronted by a Steward, a young Lascar boy in a white uniform, holding a tray full of cups of tea.

"Does Sir want tea?" He crooned.

"Er, oh yes please." Replied Jamie, he took the cup and sat on his bunk whilst politely drinking it.

The Young Steward had woken the other two boys and had given them each a cup.

One of the boys, who had told Jamie the night before, that his name was Reggie called out. "Where are you going Jamie?"

"Up on deck Reggie, it looks as though we are in for a storm, let's go and check it out."

Reggie slipped his pants on over his pyjamas, and they both hurried up to the deck.

Reggie shouted. "Holy Moley, it's a storm alright, half the boat disappears below water every time we hit a wave."

Jamie was trying to walk along the deck, but one minute he was leaning to one side, then to the other, and he was starting to feel woozy.

"I'm going down to the cabin Reggie, I'm not feeling too good." Meanwhile, Reggie was down on his hands and knees throwing up, he didn't reply, he just stayed down, moaning.

Jamie just made it to the corridor where their cabin was, when he spotted a toilet door to the right, he ran in and closed the door.

Fifteen minutes later, someone was banging on the door.

Jamie sheepishly opened it and dived into his cabin and leapt onto his bunk, moaning in pain.

Twenty four hours later, and after several attempts to make it to the dining room, he finally surfaced from the cabin, it was now fairly calm, and on reaching the dining Room, he saw Dulcie and Rachel sitting in their pre-appointed places at the long table, eating breakfast, Rachel smiled at him and asked him. "Where have you been, we missed you yesterday?"

"There was a terrible storm and I was seasick."

"Mum and I were fine, you should have come to our cabin for one of Dad's seasick tablets, if it gets rough again we will give you one."

"All three of us boys were seasick, Donald is still in bed, and Reggie has gone up on deck for some fresh air."

"Well it helps to have a Dad in the Navy, he always took these pills, and was never seasick."

Jamie wolfed down his Eggs on toast, and followed it up with more toast, there weren't many people at breakfast that day, so he ate what was not being consumed by the still seasick passengers.

"Hurry up and finish Jamie, we will be going into the Mediterranean Ocean soon, passing Gibraltar and the Moroccan Coast, you can't miss that."

"Coming, will I bring my camera up from the cabin, Rachel?"
"Yes its a clear sky, so we'll be able to see everything."

When they emerged from the staircase, She whispered to him. "Is that Reggie over by the Railing?"

"Yes, he said that he thinks you are beautiful, Rachel."

"Jamie, you can tell him that I'm taken."

"I didn't know you were taken, you should have told me first."

"Jamie it's you Idiot, I want everyone to know it's you and that's all I need." They had now sailed past the Rock, and he had taken a number of photographs. "What's the first port of call Rachel?"

"Malta, Dad was posted there once when Prince Philip was stationed there at the same time, he met him in the Officers Mess several times."

"Wow so close to Royalty, he's the Prince of Greece, he could be our Prince Consort one day."

"Really, but he's Greek?" She shook her head, then told him. "He's related to the Royal Family, so I suppose he could be.

"I'd be happy with him as a Consort."

Rachel was losing interest in the Royal family discussion, and asked. "Will you ask your cabin mates to join us two and Mum in the Lounge tonight, there is a Dance and some games as well."

"I know that they will Rachel, everyone seems to like you and your Mum, probably because you are so nice and helpful."

"Now Jamie let's go down to morning tea, I could eat an Elephant right now, this Sea breeze is so invigorating."

Malta was just as everyone expected, an amazing Island in the Mediterranean Sea, Old by any standard, it had a magnificent history, and was now host to the Mediterranean Fleet.

Rachel, Jamie and his two cabin mates explored the Island together, it was so different to England, the Locals were friendly and answered all of their questions, they thoroughly enjoyed the day.

Waving goodbye to one of natures gifts to the world, the three boys and Rachel spoke of the next port of call, Port Said in Egypt.

Rachel told the boys. "We won't be allowed on shore at Port Said, because we are travelling with Visa's, which are only recognised in British Protectorates and Commonwealth Countries."

Port Said was a very busy Port, ships coming and going through the Suez Canal stopped over for fuel and food.

Passengers could still trade with the locals, as they had boats loaded with all kinds of things for sale.

They were called Bum boats for some reason, and you had to use a rope that had a basket on the end to haul the goods up onto the deck, then if you were happy with it you could put the money in the basket and lower it down to the seller.

Rachel bought a couple things, which were barely worth the money she paid. None of the boys bought anything, they only had a few pounds to spend at the proper ports of call.

The Mooltan then took it's turn in the queue to proceed down the Suez Canal, towards the Red Sea.

Progress was slow because, when a ship is moving it causes a draft, unless it goes slowly it would cause a huge wash destroying the banks of the canal. Traffic was only one way, and groups of ships alternated in both directions.

There wasn't much to see in the Canal, just British Army vehicles, travelling along the banks, to protect the ships.

Eventually they sailed into the Red Sea adjacent to Port Suez.

The Sea is 1400 miles long and it is Bounded by Egypt, Saudi Arabia, Sudan, Eritrea, and Yemen. It took several days for the Mooltan to steam towards the entrance to the Gulf of Aden, finally docking at the Port of Aden, capital of Yemen.

The three boys and Rachel spent the day walking around Aden, it was the first time on dry land, and they had a little trouble adjusting, to their jelly legs.

Dulcie had allowed Rachel to accompany Jamie and his two cabin mates in exploring the city, she trusted Jamie and knew that both of the other boys were well brought up and would behave.

Jamie said. "There are so many beggars everywhere, most of them are children, and they seem to want cigarettes all the time."

Rachel replied. "Mum said not to give them anything, as that will attract the whole lot of them and they'd follow you all day."

Donald moaned. "Let's go back to the boat, I'm so hot and sticky, it must be a hundred degrees here, and I'm sick of these snotty nosed brats touching me all the time."

Jamie smiled and told Donald."Don't be so mean, they are poor and probably hungry, and I think they touch you because you are so White and have long Blond hair, yes they like you Donald, that one looks like a girl, here's your chance."

"I'm going back, he cried, who's coming with me?"

Rachel sang out. "Not me, I'm going to climb that Minaret in the Mosque on top of the hill."

"You can't Rachel, you're not a Muslim, they'll tell you off." shouted Reggie.

"No they won't, they allow tourists to climb them, but you must take your shoes off."

"Not likely, my Mum bought me these brand new before we left." Reggie shouted.

"Whose coming back with me?" croaked Donald.

Jamie shouted. "Donald stop being a sook, we won't be long at the Mosque, then we'll come back with you."

"OK Jamie, but promise you'll come back then, what about these dirty kids?"

"They wont bother us when we go up the Minaret."

After climbing the tower, where they could see over all of the rooftops, they descended to put their shoes back on, to the delight of Reggie, who had anticipated his being stolen.

Jamie assured him that no one would dare steal from a Mosque.

So, they slowly returned to the Ship and settled into the Lounge with cold drinks until evening, when the Mooltan slipped away from the Dock and into the Arabian Sea.

The temperature was starting to warm up and a lot of time was spent inside, mostly in the Library by the four teenagers, and when Dulcie ventured out of her cabin and up stairs, they would join her in the Lounge.

The next port of call was Colombo, that little tear drop hanging below India.

In fact it is actually joined to the Southern tip of India, but it is a separate country and a British Protectorate.

The Mooltan docked in Colombo Harbour early in the morning, Dulcie and Rachel had arranged with Jamie to meet at the gangplank and they left the ship before most other passengers. She had arranged for the two teenagers to go on an Elephant ride. They took a taxi to the Compound, where Jamie looked up at the huge beast, and smiled at it, the Mahout got it to sit and a wary Jamie carefully climbed aboard.

"Piece of cake Rachel, just do what I did." He shouted.

"I don't think I can look as scared as you did Jamie, and I certainly can't shake like that."

"At least I'm on mine, you haven't even tried it yet."

Rachel swiftly mounted her Animal and lead them both off down the beach. "Wait on Rachel. I've got to turn it round, giddy up Dumbo." he shouted. Dulcie was almost in tears watching, and listening to London's version of Sabu the Elephant boy.

Eventually his animal just followed Rachel's without any instructions from Jamie, the poor animal had been doing this for years.

There was a Lake just a few hundred feet away from the beach, both of the animals headed for it and drank heartily, then Jamie's Mount turned it's trunk on him and squirted a little of the water on his head.

"I must have really annoyed it, I'll just shut up and let it do what it wants."

They spent about an hour with the Elephants, taking photo's, both on and off the beasts, Rachel actually cuddled hers and it lifted her up onto its back, she called out to Jamie. "Just get close to Jumbo and give him a cuddle, then he'll treat you like a brother."

Jumbo did just that, he turned to Jamie and squirted more water over him.

He was now soaking wet, Rachel and Dulcie were laughing so much that they were in stitches.

When they returned to the Compound, they paid the Mahout, and Dulcie tipped him as well, then they took another taxi to Lavinia Beach, where they were to meet Reggie and Donald.

The boys saw them coming and quickly changed into their bathers, before the ladies got too close, as there were no change rooms there, they paraded around with the long thin surfboards that the native children used.

Jamie saw them and laughed. "You don't know how to Surf, there's no beaches in London Reggie."

"Can so, Jamie you just watch me." And he ran into the placid Colombo water. Jamie shouted. "There's no surf Reggie, you'll just sink."

Donald dropped his board and stood and stared at his mate, who was now desperately trying to retrieve his board, what little waves there were had taken it away from him.

All of them were laughing at Reggie, Dulcie had her camera out and had taken enough photos to embarrass him later.

Donald and Jamie dived into the water and helped him get the board back. Reggie grumbled. "There's no cord to tie to your ankle, that's why I lost it."

Rachel cackled. "Reggie, come on you've never surfed before have you?"

"Well no not really, but I saw a picture of an Australian surfer once,"

Dulcie spoke seriously."Put all of the Boards back up the beach, and leave them alone, then you can all go for a swim, that is if you boys can swim."

Reggie and Donald meekly got into the water and dog paddled around trying to impress Rachel, she smiled condescendingly, then took Donald's arm and showed him how to do the breast stroke, Reggie copied them and they now at least knew how to swim in theory.

Jamie, realising that he had the ascendancy, because he was a fairly good swimmer, gave them a little lesson in the breast stroke, and his version of the Australian crawl.

"OK Jamie, that's enough, we know that you can swim like Johnny Weissmuller, but I bet you can't surf either." Reggie moaned.

"No I can't but I didn't pretend that I could like you Reggie."

They spent the next couple of hours on the beach, getting sunburnt, then it was time to return to the boat, Dulcie suggested that they walk back, so that they could see how the locals lived.

It wasn't long before they were walking between the tiny temporary houses, when suddenly an Elephant appeared in front of them. Donald screamed. "Look out it'll kill us all." And he ran off down a side street.

They burst out laughing at him, as the animal was quite tame and it just turned slowly around and strolled away, apparently they wander around by themselves all day looking for food and drink, a little like the Cows in India.

Rachel was thinking to herself. "It is going to be fun at dinner this evening, what with Jamie and Jumbo, then Reggie and the Surfing, to be topped off with Donald nearly being killed by a huge beast."

The walk home was made light by the chatter between the group, they had all enjoyed the day in Colombo.

That evening, after Dinner amid the continued banter and laughter about the days adventures, the Mooltan continued on it's way towards Fremantle, Australia.

Two days out and, they were about to cross the Equator, the ships crew took on a strange appearance, they had changed into different clothes, and towards evening, some of the passengers, being those who had never crossed the Equator before were gathered on deck, where they were all told that they were Polliwogs, then King Neptune arrived with his assistants, waiving fish at the Polliwogs, asking them to kiss the fish, then dousing them with sea water, and after an hilarious time, finally announcing that they were all now, Shell Backs, and fully qualified sailors.

Dulcie and the teenagers took part in the ceremony, enjoying the fun involved, then they paraded around, proud to be official seafarers.

The Party went into the early hours, and a great deal of the Crew and Passengers had hangovers the next morning.

Most passengers sat around the deck and enjoyed the calm seas, soaking up the sunshine, and watching the Porpoises escorting the Ship.

Jamie and Rachel were starting to get excited, a few days time and they would be in Fremantle, Australia. Both were wondering what it would be like, the long voyage would be over, as all they had to do now was circumnavigate the Southern part of Australia to Sydney.

Jamie asked Donald and Reggie, where they were getting off the Ship? Reggie said "Melbourne, my Uncle lives in Collingwood, so I've got to barrack for the Magpies Football team."

"Is that an Australian Rules team Reggie."

"Yes Jamie, they are the best, so my Uncle says, they wear black and white jumpers."

Donald said. "I'm getting off at Port Adelaide, My Mum and Dad came out last year and he has a job as a Grounds man at the Adelaide Oval."

Jamie offered. "You'll get to see lots of Cricket then for free."

He replied. "Yes we've got a Test Match this year. So I'll be able to sit in the stand everyday."

Rachel told the boys. "Let's all have a fun time in Fremantle as it will be our last Port together.

They all agreed to go into Fremantle early, to see as much as they could, take lots of photos, and swap each others new addresses.


The Mooltan docked at Six in the morning, by nine o'clock most passengers were being bussed into the city. Rachel and the three boys were on the first bus, they spent the whole day in Freo, in and out of the shops, buying food and drinks, a lot of lemonade and juice, they even had a milkshake, which was something new to them all.

The most interesting place was the Fremantle Jail, it was no longer in use and was open to visitors, they spent a couple of hours in jail that day. Pretending to be Convicts.

They rode the last bus back to the ship.

Then lined the deck to wave goodbye to Freo, and they were now talking about what to do in Adelaide.

The Weather, the Ocean, in fact everything had been great, including the good food, plenty of drinks and a lot of fun aboard ship, from the Red Sea all the way to Freo.

The passage to Adelaide was sometimes a little bit different to the previous part of the journey.

They sailed down the Indian Ocean to the Southwest tip of Western Australia, it was calm until they reached Augusta, as they turned left into the Australian Bight, everything changed, within minutes a huge Gale was blowing from the Southern Ocean, tossing the Mooltan around like a top, the wind was howling and the ship was behaving just like it had in the Bay of Biscay.

Dulcie shared the seasick tablets with the boys, and all except poor Donald were OK, he had to go to the cabin and lay down.

The other's were sitting in the Lounge eating and drinking all by themselves, as most of the passengers were doing the same as Donald.

Everybody on board was relieved to dock at Port Adelaide, for most of them, the only time that the Mooltan had been livable for the last two days.

They said goodbye to Donald who was more than happy to leave the ship, he was greeted by his Parents, having introduced them to the others, they all agreed to exchange addresses, and write to each other.

Donald's Dad offered to drive them into The City, he dropped them off outside a Cafe, they all wanted to try more Milkshakes.

Adelaide is known as the City of Churches, that became very obvious as the three teenagers investigated the town centre.

Jamie had sought out the Adelaide Zoo, so they spent most of the day there, because none of them were interested in Churches, and they were unaware that it was also famous for it's Pubs.

At the end of the day, they caught the train back to Port Adelaide, and boarded the Ship once more.

Dulcie gave them more tablets, as the weather forecast was not good for the trip to Melbourne.

The Bight turned on one of it's best storms for a long time, the crew told the passengers that more ships had run aground there than on the Skeleton Coast in Africa, this of course wasn't quite true but it made everyone aboard look forward to steaming into Port Phillip Bay, where it was usually calm, and the Passengers could relax and enjoy the view on each side of the Bay.

Docking at Station Pier, Port Melbourne, where Reggie's Uncle Bert, wearing a black and white striped football jumper, met him and, without saying too much, told him to throw his bags in the back of the Old Ford Utility, and jump in next to his Dog, that was laying on the floor by the only seat.

They waved goodbye to Reggie, as the vehicle disappeared along the Esplanade, never to be seen or contacted by his two friends again.

Dulcie, Rachel and Jamie caught the train into Spencer Street Station, which was right in the centre of the City of Melbourne, they walked down from the entrance of the station, under the clocks, to the pavement and started to cross the road.

The sharp blast of a whistle pulled them up in their tracks, A very tall policeman approached them and took them aside, while the rest of the pedestrians, who were patiently waiting for the lights to change to green, smiled at them.

The officer spoke. "Madam, you were jay walking across the busiest junction in Melbourne, I can fine you, but I think that you might be new to the city, is that so?"

Dulcie quivered, then answered, Yes Officer we have just arrived from London, the boat is at Port Melbourne"

He replied. "Take this as a warning, I will let you off today, now you take care Madam."

He went back to waving his arms in several directions, instructing other wayward souls, who might also try to break the road laws.

Jamie whispered. "We don't bother about lights in London, we just cross the road when we want, and just dodge the cars and buses."

Rachel said. "Well it's obvious that they don't do that here, and it will possibly be the same in Sydney."

It put a slight dampener on their day, but they found a lovely cafe in the Myers Store, just up the road, they sat and drank tea and ate cakes and looked and listened to the locals.

"They've go funny accents, haven't they Rachel?"

"Not all of them Jamie, there are a lot of educated people in the cities."

Dulcie corrected her. "Rachel, just because some of them speak with a strong accent, doesn't mean that they are uneducated."

"Mum, I didn't really mean that, but they do speak differently to us."

"Rachel, Nearly everyone in England speaks differently to you and me, so you will just have to learn to understand everyone."

Jamie chimed in with. "Well at least everyone speaks the same language here." He looked up to see two young Asian girls walking towards them, one of them had seen him staring at her, as she passed, she said something to him.

He continued to look at them as they walked past, he sat open mouthed, he had not understood a word that the girl had said to him, he looked at Dulcie and shrugged.

She smiled at him and told him. "It sounded a little bit like Taiwanese Jamie, we are much closer to Asia than England, and you shouldn't have been staring at them."

"I know Dulcie, but that girl did look nice, even though she had funny shaped eyes."

This was immediately followed by the toe of Rachel's shoe being kicked hard against his shin.

"Ouch! Rachel, what was that for, I was only looking?"

"You are going to be in trouble if you ever go to an Asian country, Jamie."

"You jealous Rachel" he squeaked.

"No!" she boomed.

He mumbled, under his breath. "Thought you might dump me."

"I heard that Jamie Dexter, I'm not jealous, It's just that you shouldn't stare at any girls, while I'm with you."

Dulcie intervened with. "Someone needs to make up their mind."

Both Jamie and Rachel looked down at their plates, both were trying to avoid being seen blushing.

"I think we all need some fresh air now, children."

They were relieved to be out in the open now, every time a female approached them, Jamie looked down at the pavement smiling to himself.

Rachel, just hooked her arm under his and smooched up to him, giggling like mad "You are such a clown Jamie, OK, just look, but no staring, Right?"

This evoked a huge smile from him, and he blew her a fake kiss. Now all three were happy again.

They were having to make all sorts of adjustments in just a couple of hours while in Melbourne.

Rachel told Jamie. "Sydney is bigger than this place, and it is more cosmopolitan, so they say."

"Let's go back to Flinders Street Station and cross the road with all of the other people, then catch our train to Port Melbourne please?" Complained Dulcie.

Rachel replied. "I'm all for that Mum, my feet are killing me, walking on these hard pavements, after the wooden decks on the ship."

Sailing out of Port Melbourne was quite interesting, as they had to use a Tug to negotiate them from the Wharf, there was a lot of boat traffic, with cargo ships and the Mooltan queuing to go up the Bay, towards the Rip, and then into Bass Strait, turn left towards the South Pacific Ocean, past Cape Howe, and sail North, eventually past Botany Bay and then enter the Heads.

There was so much going on in Sydney Harbour, with fishing craft, yachts, Cargo vessels and Naval craft all going in different direction, distracting from the magnificent scenery surrounding the vast expanse of water as they passed Kirribilli Point they saw the many Ferries in and out of South Quay.

It was too much for them to take in all at once, they kept drawing each others attention to whatever they were looking at, eventually everyone was taken in by the sight of the Magnificent Sydney Harbour Bridge, as it slowly loomed above them while the Mooltan glided beneath it as she rounded Dawes Point, then was gently nestled into the wharf by Tugs.

While they were waiting to go through Customs, Dulcie saw Eric Widmark in the crowd of Sydney siders waiting to greet their loved ones, they were all waving at each other, Rachel squealed, she was so excited to see her Dad again, Jamie saw him and smiled, this man was to become his surrogate Dad from now on.

They didn't have to wait long, there were hugs and kisses all round, Jamie had to settle for a handshake, but it was accompanied by a huge smile from Eric.

He ushered them down to the VIP parking area, where he showed them his Buick Eight, a very large American Limousine.

Then he drove them to Point Piper, an Elite Suburb, he parked the Buick in the Driveway, the new arrivals sat and admired the expensive looking house, Dulcie asked. "Did you actually buy this mansion, Eric?"

"I put a deposit on it dear, we can pay it off quite easily with my current Salary."

Rachel squealed. "I love it Dad, I bet it's gorgeous inside."

Jamie was stunned, the House was just like the Mansion in Etchingham, it stood on a hill overlooking the Harbour, he could see right across to the other side of the water, there were several Warships tied up there, he asked Eric. "Sir, are those ships still in commission."

"Some of them are Jamie, the large Aircraft Carrier is the HMAS Melbourne."

Dulcie grouched. "Eric we are here to see our new home, not inspect the Fleet, honestly, you men only have one thing on your mind."

"Oh! Oh! Jamie, I think we are in trouble, so let's go inside, come Ladies." They inspected the house inside and outside, chatting about who would have which room, and whose job it would be to mow the vast lawn, etcetera.

After they were all acquainted with their new home, Eric drove them to the Hotel where they would be staying until they had been given the title to the House and could move in.

That night, after Dinner, Eric told His Daughter and Jamie that he had already enrolled them in the local High School.

Dulcie wanted to know why they weren't going to an Elite Private School.

He explained to her. "Dulcie, none of our families have been to Private schools, Ted Dexter attained the Rank of Major, he went to Greenwich Secondary School, Robertson also went to a Secondary school, and I have done pretty well being educated at Tonbridge Wells Secondary. Elite Church Schools fill their heads with egotistical rubbish, including unnecessary Religious nonsense, and they breed arrogance, both Rachel and Jamie are A students and will be more than capable of handling a little toughness, should it come there way, also it will be character building."

After further discussion, they all agreed that it was for the best, they would spend their last two years in State school, Matriculate and then go to a good University, Rachel was keen to do Medicine, Jamie was still unsettled about his future, but he was open to suggestions from his new Mum and Dad. He felt sure that the advice would be good.

After the long six weeks voyage on the Mooltan, they were glad to be able to relax and look forward to discovering everything about their new home town of Sydney, Australia.